GIFTED

Robert Horsey

Editor: Terrie M. Scott
Cover Art: Terrie M. Scott

ISBN-13: 978-0692963067
ISBN-10: 0692963065

Printed in the United States of America

www.gifted-thenovel.com

For

Courtney Dorney

You've been my inspiration from day one.

Never forget…you will always be my "Carolina."

Acknowledgements

GIFTED is a story that has been brewing in my head for many years; inspired by my time spent working at Mid-America Transplant Services in St. Louis, Missouri. This is a fictional story based, loosely, on my experiences there as an Organ Procurement Coordinator. During this time in my career, I had the extreme honor of working with donor families as they navigated the waters of grief and the unexpected loss of their loved one. I was allowed into their lives during what would seem to be their most devastating and vulnerable moments. The compassion that they were able to muster is the reason for this story. It was written as a tribute to each of them and the thousands of donor families around the country that provide the gift of life through the selfless act of organ and tissue donation.

I'd also like to thank my friends and former colleagues from that organization for imparting upon me this wonderful and fulfilling career; specifically, Brian Scheller, RN, CPTC and Diane Brockmeier, the current President and CEO. In addition, I'd like to thank the numerous (too many to name here) other colleagues with whom I've worked and learned from since then. My career in the field of nursing and organ transplantation would not have been possible without you.

There are a few people who deserve special recognition for their guidance in this endeavor, which I was nervous and reluctant to begin. I have learned that the path to writing is littered with obstacles such as uncertainty, self-doubt and procrastination. Padraig Reynolds, a former high school buddy turned successful screenwriter and director (*Rites of Spring* and *The Devil's Dolls*), encouraged me early on to "just write it". That sound and simple advice inspired me to first write a screenplay and then this novel. Without his initial encouragement, I surely wouldn't be writing this Acknowledgment Page. I must also recognize the International and New York Times Best-Selling Author, Colin Campbell (*Free*

Days with George). Several phone conversations with him regarding content and creative writing helped keep me on track while bringing this project to fruition – thanks, Colin – PROST!! My editor and cover artist, Terrie M. Scott, deserves a special degree of thanks for her tolerance and patience with me as a first-time novelist. Her editing was superb and her cover artwork was, as you can see, excellent. All my best for your future endeavors, Terrie.

A sincere thank you to my friends and family that have struggled through the first few iterations of this book. Your honest, and sometimes brutal, feedback has helped shape this into the book that it has become.

Finally, I must acknowledge the unending support of my girlfriend, (as a fifty-year-old novelist, I choke on that word) Courtney and her two sons, Michael and Ozzy. In addition, I must thank her parents, Mike and Mary Dorney. Without this tribe of backers in my corner cheering me and supporting my work, I don't know that I would have completed this journey. Your love and support will always be with me, just as my never-ending gratitude is with you.

PROLOGUE

SIX DAYS EARLIER

The Mills' residence is a spacious four-bedroom, three-and-a-half-bath, two-story Tudor style; their home for two years now. It sits on a cul-de-sac within a posh, newer neighborhood in the suburban area just South of St. Louis, Missouri. It is way more house than Kevin and Sherry need at the moment, but it's meant to be "grown into." From the outside looking in, their lives *seemed* to be perfect.

Kevin Mills is a handsome, athletic and earnest man of thirty-two years. He graduated from a four-year nursing program (one semester early), with honors. He felt a calling, early on, toward a career in healthcare, specifically the field of organ transplant. This passion grew from watching his closest childhood friend succumb to a viral heart disease at the young age of sixteen, after languishing on the heart transplant list.

His nursing career began as a critical care nurse in a Level-One, Trauma Intensive Care Unit; the largest of its kind in the state of Missouri. As a Level-One ICU, they see the worst, of the worst. The deathly ill and mortally injured are brought here for advanced healthcare. As a corollary, the best, of the best, are chosen to work in this fast-paced and high-stress environment.

Kevin was the tip of the spear working in the ICU. He was drawn toward those patients who survived the nastiest of accidents and had the most complex of injuries. As a result, he was frequently chosen to care for those unique patients who would occasionally go on to become organ donors as a result of their devastating injuries. It was his previous life experience that fueled his desire to help make the best out of these particular situations, for everyone involved.

His abilities to critically think through complex situations and to skillfully manage his patient's care (with the precision that rivals any of the physician interns) were readily recognized by the organ procurement coordinators that frequented the Trauma ICU. For that reason, Kevin was recruited to join their specialized team. Four years later, he is now a nationally-credentialed and well-respected leader at Missouri Donor Network, the Organ Procurement Organization that services the state of Missouri. The nature of his job is not necessarily physical. It's not like he's working the pavement of the Missouri highway system in the blazing hot August heat. The most physically demanding part of his job would be staying awake for twenty-four to thirty-six hours at a time when working on a donor case –

still no easy chore. What makes his job especially hard is the pressure of knowing that every little thing you do, every decision you make in the management of an organ donor, can affect the lives of so many people. One organ donor can save the lives of up to eight different people and positively impact everyone around them. For this reason, Kevin, and those who do his job are under an intense amount of pressure to get it right, with no mistakes. Lives are on the line every time that pager goes off.

Sherry Mills is a tall spectacle of class and poise. She hails from an extremely well-healed family on the West side of St. Louis County. She learned, from her father, the principles of hard work and from her mother she learned the value and importance of family. Sherry's beauty is a point of pride for her and she uses it to her advantage as a pharmaceutical sales representative. With her looks and charming personality all packaged up in a business suit and an over-sized Louis Vuitton bag on her arm, she could sell garlic to a vampire.

They were earning more than enough money to support a family. Their careers were in place, the house was in place but still no family of their own. They agreed, at the beginning, that they should wait until they had purchased a house rather than starting a family inside their little one-bedroom apartment in downtown St. Louis. Sherry had been patient for the first two years of their three-year marriage. However, this past year, she had been pushing harder and harder on Kevin to agree that now was the right time. It wasn't that he didn't want to have a family, he wanted to very much. The issue that stood in the way was Kevin's work schedule. In the business of clinical organ procurement, the concept of a "9 to 5er" simply doesn't exist. The hours worked are random, long and very unpredictable. It wouldn't be uncommon for Kevin to get called to work on a case in the morning and not return home until the afternoon of the next day. His was a grueling schedule with no consistency.

When the controversy surfaces, and it does regularly, Sherry commonly reminds him of the many missed Sunday dinners with her parents, birthday celebrations and the occasional holiday. The proverbial straw that broke the camel's back occurred this past October 31st. Halloween has always been her favorite holiday, ever since she was a young girl. Sherry loves to ghoulishly decorate the house and dress up in a scary witch's costume - wart nose make-up and oversized pointy hat included - to hand out candy to the neighborhood kids. Like most things in her life, only the best will do – big candy bars for everyone. In fact, she pushed for the house they live in with that date in mind, it's perfect because of its prime location on the circle and the neighborhood full of kids. Her house would be the favorite house among the kids in costume each year, and she saw to it.

As they were dressing for the occasion that night, Kevin's pager, that obnoxious noisemaker, chirped; she immediately knew her evening was going to be ruined. He was asked to go to work on his day off due to a heavy caseload. Most people would have said no to that request, however, Kevin's career and his commitment to saving lives took priority over costumes and candy. That particular night he went on a local donor management case. She didn't see him again until the morning of November 2nd.

Sherry realized, and later insisted, that if they were to start their family it would not work with him having that job and those hours. She was firm on this, and it became a point of contention that caused many fights. Their "perfect little home" was beginning to feel like a big empty house for Sherry.

It was early on a cool winter's evening. The sun had disappeared behind the earth a few hours earlier. Kevin was making his way back home after one of those marathon cases. As he pulled his 5-series BMW into the driveway, he noticed that the lights were out downstairs but caught a faint glimpse of light through one of the upstairs windows.

11

Kevin said in a subdued voice, to himself, "I'm in the doghouse."

He, wearily, entered the front door of their well-appointed home and walked past the ten by fourteen wedding day portrait that greets all their visitors. He announced his entrance, "Sherry, I'm home!"

Normally, the first to greet him would be their yappy lap dog, whom Kevin secretly despised. His eight-pound body frame certainly didn't fit the name that they had compromised on, Thor. If Kevin has his way, their next dog will be an Old English Bull Dog, pushing eighty pounds; to be named later, by compromise, of course.

Silence. No yappy dog. Kevin thought this was peculiar, but pressed on. He continued to make his way through the dark spacious first level declaring his arrival in a confused but playful voice, "Hey babe, where are you?"

Kevin noticed the illumination of the hallway at the top of the stairs bleeding down into the living room. He climbed the oversized stairs and turned the corner to see the French-style doors to their bedroom wide open and the lights on. As he entered the room, he said, "Sherry, are you up here?" Her absence and the sight of the open dresser drawers, the open closet doors and articles of her clothing scattered about the usually clean and organized room could mean only one thing. He exclaimed, "NO, NO, NO! She didn't!"

Sherry was gone.

Kevin rapidly made his way down the stairs, through the living room and into the kitchen. He flipped on the lights to their gourmet kitchen to reveal exactly what he was afraid of finding one of these days, the envelope. It was addressed simply to "KEV". He snatched it from the granite countertop of the large island and ripped it open. When removing the hand-written letter, a sonogram image of a fetus fell onto the counter. He picked it up and examined it. "What is this," he wondered aloud. He, then, turned his attention back to the letter.

It read:

> *"Dear Kevin,*
> *I know what you're thinking. But, no it's not ours. My <u>YOUNGER</u> sister is now expecting their second child. This is supposed to be happening for us.*
> *Just over three years ago, we vowed to each other in front of our families and God that our relationship and marriage would always come first. We agreed that starting a family was what we both wanted. You have not held up your end of that agreement. I've grown tired of taking a backseat to your career.*
> *I'm sure this comes as no surprise to you, as we have been arguing about this for months. I am leaving you. I even told you how I would do it to get your attention, which obviously didn't have an impact on you. I HAVE OPTIONS!*

*Know that I am heartbroken by this! I do care
about you and about us, but we need this time apart.*
    *So, you don't worry about where I am, I'll be at
my parent's home. Please don't try to contact me, it
will just muddy the waters. I need time and space.
Please respect that.*
    Yours?
    Sher"

"What the hell does she mean by options?" he said aloud. Shock took over. His knees buckled and he spun at the waist so that his back was able to slide down against the island, to the floor. He dropped his head into his hands and began to cry. The house was silent except for his grief.

CHAPTER 1

Brilliant light engulfs the sterile room filled with members of three different surgical teams. The surgeons, dressed in sterile blue gowns, crowd around the operating table at the center of the room. This table is illuminated by even brighter lights, which hang from the ceiling above it. The surgeons are working independently of each other, yet in concert, to achieve their common goal. They have assembled in this Kansas City, Missouri operating room to procure their respective organs from this extremely unfortunate accident victim, thanks to the unselfish generosity of his poor widow; she consented to the donation of his organs.

A local liver transplant surgeon and his second-year surgical resident are working in the abdominal cavity preparing to recover the liver, pancreas, both kidneys and the small intestines for transplant into several local organ recipients. The lung surgeon traveled, by air, from Chicago to procure his organs for a blessed transplant recipient waiting back home for her new lease on life to begin once she receives her life-saving double lung transplant. The heart recovery team has flown in from St. Louis, Missouri, a mere two-hundred-thirty-eight-mile trip, to procure their organ.

This three-man surgical crew, consisting of Kevin Mills, Dr. Sanji Sandau and his third-year surgical fellow, have made many trips like this together. This one is a relatively quick jaunt compared the four-hour roundtrip flight they had the previous day to a small town in northern Minnesota.

Kevin Mills is dressed in light green scrubs. His surgical mask is up over his mouth and nose and he has on a tight fitting surgical cap, that is covering his disheveled hair. He stands near and behind his surgeon, Dr. Sandau. Kevin is outside the sterile circle that crowds around the operating table, so there's no need for him to be scrubbed in and gowned at this time. He is poised, at the ready, to start the flush line hanging from the tall IV pole before him. Kevin tries to focus on the task at hand, however his deep blue eyes reveal a wandering mind.

Dr. Sandau, from the operating table inside the circle, voices his instruction in a heavy Indian accent, "Kevin, you can start the flush line now."

Kevin stands in silence with his hand on the roller clamp. His attention is outside that room. No response.

Dr. Sandau turns his head and repeats the order. His voice has taken on a stern tone, "Kevin, the flush. The cross clamp is on."

Snapping out of his daze, Kevin rolls the clamp open and watches as the frigid preservation solution begins to run into the drip chamber of the flush line leading to the donor. He's back in the present. "Sorry doc, it's open and running to you now."

"Yeah, the heart is flushing nicely now. Let's run in all three liters."

Kevin replies, "Sounds good. I'll scrub in after the flush."

"Perfect. It's looking good, so far," Dr. Sandau reports.

Kevin makes his way out of the operating room and into a much smaller anteroom, where the scrub sinks are located. He stands tall, scouring his hands and forearms with a sterile scrub brush as he stares straight forward, at nothing. Again, his eyes reveal his drifting mind playing out his recent life changing event. His eyes begin to brim with tears as he moves his arms and hands under the warm running water, removing the last of the soapy suds. He shakes his head clear of these thoughts as he turns the water off by touching his knee to the scrub sink basin. "Pull it together, man," he whispers to himself.

Kevin backs his way through the operating room door. His hands are raised out in front of him as he turns toward the waiting OR scrub tech, who hands him a sterile towel. He uses it to dry his hands up to his elbows; careful not to contaminate his now sterile skin. The tech, then, assists him in donning his blue sterile gown and gloves. Now, with proper OR attire on, Kevin makes his way through the maze of medical talent that fills that operating room and into the sterile circle. As he approaches the back table where Dr. Sandau and his surgical fellow are inspecting the heart that was just procured from the organ donor, he catches them in mid-conversation.

Dr. Sandau, a brilliant man, is the consummate teacher. Applying a small sterile ruler to the vascular tissue, he educates his young colleague, "You see here, this aortic cuff is a near perfect caliber for our recipient, very little trimming will be needed." Running his fingers along the visible path of the coronary arteries that line the outside of the heart, he continues, "These are pristine."

Kevin arrives at the back table and interrupts, "Is this heart going to work for you, Dr. Sandau?"

"It should be just fine. Can you finish getting this packaged up for us?"

"I'll take it from here, doc," he replied.

"Thanks. I need to make a call back to the hospital."

Kevin says, "I'll meet you both back at the ambulance. It shouldn't be more than a fifteen-minute ride to the airport, with lights and sirens and only a fifty-minute flight back home; we'll have the tail wind." The two surgeons break scrub as Kevin continues to diligently and professionally package up the organ for safe travel back home to St. Louis, just as he has hundreds of times before.

The cabin lights are dimmed in the rented eight-passenger Learjet as it streaks through the cold night air. Dr. Sandau and Kevin sit directly across the aisle from one another in the second row. On the floor, secured tightly between Kevin's feet, is a cooler appropriately labeled, "HUMAN ORGAN." The third member of the fly-out team that night, the surgical fellow, is sprawled out in the back row of the plane sleeping soundly.

"Wow, that guy can sleep anywhere," Kevin said.

"You know what they say - eat when you can, sleep when you can." Dr. Sandau belly laughs at his comment while Kevin musters up only a half grin. "You seem a bit off tonight, Kevin."

"Well, you know how I feel about flying."

Waving off Kevin's reply, "No, not that. In the OR, there's no room for error in what we do. Time is tissue."

"Yeah, sorry about that, Sanji. Things are no better at home."

"Sherry's still gone?"

"Yeah," Kevin replied.

"Does she truly understand what you do, what it takes?"

"I had this job long before we ever met, so yeah, she knew the demands of it before we got married. It's still the whole having-kids-now thing," Kevin explained.

"I'm really sorry that you're going through this, Kevin. Have you been able to talk since she left?"

"Not much. I'm trying to give her the space that she asked for, but it's killing me." His emotions begin breaking through. "I love her so much," Kevin professes.

Dr. Sandau pauses momentarily and considers the possibly of overstepping his boundaries. He pushes on anyway, "Believe me, I truly understand the importance of family. I wouldn't be where I am today without my own. I hope your wife realizes that it's possible to have both."

"That's the problem, I don't think she believes it. She doesn't want to do it – well, to use her word, alone," Kevin replied.

Sanji continues, "The career path that you have chosen is so vitally important. She needs to know that in order for her to appreciate it." Dr. Sandau gestures to the cooler between Kevin's feet, "Take that heart for example. You've never met the man that will get that heart tonight and you probably never will. But, you're out here in the middle of the night, risking your life on this plane in order to help save his. Know this, your work has changed his life and the lives of his entire family, forever."

20

"Thanks, doc," Kevin replied. "I'm sure she knows that, but I guess she's just lost sight of it."

"Listen, I've been in the transplant game for a long time and I have worked with many coordinators, but none like you. It's such a relief to not have to worry about the process or the logistics of coordinating the transplant when I know you're on the case with me."

A proud smile appears on Kevin's face. "Wow, you're really buttering me up."

"Well, it's true," Sanji continues. "I can't tell you how much stress that takes off of me."

A pride-filled warmth wells up in Kevin's chest as he listens to these words of recognition for his hard work coming from a man that he admires – someone understands. With a slight chuckle, he says, "I should have you talk to Sherry."

Dr. Sandau laughs loudly, "I will if you think it would help."

"I'll keep your number on speed dial."

The co-pilot leans back through the open door of the cockpit to address the passengers in a loud voice, "Excuse me, guys. We're about twenty minutes to touchdown in St. Louis. Dr. Sandau, your helicopter is waiting at the airport to take you to University Hospital."

Dr. Sandau leans across the aisle and says to Kevin,

"See what I mean, you're always one step ahead."

"That's how I roll," Kevin laughs.

The glow from the instrumentation panel shines through the darkened cabin. The conversation exchange between the co-pilot and the control tower can easily be heard. Speaking into his microphone, the co-pilot says, "Spirit of St. Louis Airfield control tower, this is Echo-Charlie-Tango-Two-Four-Seven requesting clearance for landing with life-flight status. We have six souls aboard. Over."

The radio squelches and a loud voice is heard through the cockpit speaker, "Roger, Echo-Charlie-Tango-Two-Four-Seven. This is Spirit of St. Louis Control. You have clearance to land on runway one with life-flight status. Air traffic is being diverted. Over."

That loud exchange and the shuffling of his co-passengers wakes the surgical fellow from his over-worked induced sleep. He sits upright, looking confused. "Did he just say six souls aboard this plane? Did we pick somebody up mid-flight or something?"

Kevin reaches down between his feet and grabs the cooler. He turns to face the young doctor in the back of the plane, lifts the cooler over his head and says, "Six souls; here's the sixth life at stake."

CHAPTER 2

The Forum City Diner is a twenty-four/seven local landmark known for serving greasy sliders and indigestion. It's ideally located near two large hospital complexes and the confluence of three major interstate highways in Downtown St. Louis.

Loretta Stone is a hard-working, hard-charging, late-thirties African-American woman. She's been slinging coffee and serving up that diner's indigestion for nearly three years. After the sudden death of her husband, she was forced to get a job there to support their two young sons, JT and Mikey. James was his name; the unfortunate victim of his own lifestyle and bad genes. Diabetes, hypertension, obesity, smoking and other overindulgent behaviors caught up with him. He died from a heart attack at the age of thirty-three.

They were high school sweethearts, not exactly the king and queen of the prom but they were young and in love. It was the Fall of their Senior year when their lives were changed forever by the conception of their first, James Thomas – they would call him JT. Loretta spent the remainder of that school year as a pregnant teenager, and thus, fodder for all the gossip mongers; fellow students, parents and teachers alike. This hardened her in some ways, making her tough on the outside. She and James were forced to grow up quickly – too quickly in fact, missing out on much of the joy that one's last year in high school should bring. Friday night football games, pep rallies and weekend parties were replaced with baby preparations, prenatal vitamins and jobs in order to support their new-comer.

Upon graduating from high school, they were married in a civil ceremony which was attend only by each of their best friends. Their parent's official permission for the union was received, but under protest; none of them attended it. Shortly after, James landed a very nice day job working construction. The pay was decent, but the health benefits were what saved her from future bankruptcy. Loretta supplemented their income with a part-time job working at a nearby daycare center.

She and James used to joke that working with the kids while she was pregnant was considered "on-the-job training." She worked right up until she brought JT into this world, kicking and screaming.

Upon completion of her maternity leave, she and James decided that she would not return to work and that she should just focus on raising the kid. Besides, they couldn't really afford childcare even with the discount she would get at the day care center.

JT's brother, Mikey, was born nine years later. Not exactly a planned addition, but a welcomed one nonetheless. With the addition to their family and a few extra dollars in the bank, it was necessary and possible to move into a three-bedroom apartment; however, still in a shady area of downtown St. Louis. Things were going well enough for the growing Stone family, better than either of them had predicted a decade earlier.

James had just over fifteen years at his construction job and, as a result, became quite skilled at his craft. Because of near perfect attendance and an admirable work ethic, he was promoted up through the ranks. He was a Foreman when he died. The loss of his income and benefits was a financial disaster for Loretta and her two boys, then, fifteen and six years old. She knew that her days as a stay-at-home mom were over. At the time of her widowing, with a high school diploma and no formal training, her career options were limited at best. She considered returning to the day care center, but knew that wouldn't be enough to support the three of them. Once the dust had settled from reconciling James' affairs, she quickly found work at the Forum City Diner. Currently, she manages to work thirty to forty hours a week barely making ends meet, leaving little wiggle room. She's a woman whose faith has been tested, yet she has the heart of a disciple. She will go without so that her sons have the things they need, and occasionally the things they want.

To nearly all outsiders, Loretta appears a bit worn down by her life. On most days, she wears her tattered and frumpy waitress uniform and no make-up, because who's got time for that.

While rinsing her hands in the old dingy sink of the diner bathroom, she finds herself staring deeply into her own eyes; her reflection in the mirror. The bright lights of the bathroom reveal the obvious fatigue in her dark eyes. She musters up a fake smile and mutters, "Okay, Lo, if it don't start it will never end."

The diner is filled this morning with a diverse crowd; drowsy truck drivers pulling in off the road, business men and women from the many downtown high-rises conducting their Friday morning meetings and a smattering of healthcare workers from the nearby hospitals. Loretta hustles around the diner providing the best service that she can for her patrons and her tough boss. The tips are what pay her bills, her lifeline. While clearing dishes from one of her corner booths, she finds her prize – a single dollar bill and some loose change; a disappointment to say the least. Her expectations were high from that group because they were all dressed in suits, even the young serf taking notes. She picks up the gratuity and crams it into her apron pocket and whispers to herself, "Just a couple more years, then this is a memory." Loretta has a plan for her future, one that has nothing to do with hustling for other people's spare change.

The counter seating is usually reserved for those frequent flyers of the diner. Sitting in his favorite spot, near the end of the row, is Kevin Mills. He's looking weary as ever in his all-too-familiar pair of surgical scrubs. His messenger bag and white lab coat occupy the vacant seat to his right. A picked over short stack, smothered in a mixed berry compote, sits in front of him. His wedding ring is off its reserved finger and he's spinning it like a top on the counter, contemplating his relative life situation.

Loretta makes her way down the business side of the counter with a pot of coffee in each hand, leaded and unleaded. Without much conversation, because the regulars know the system and she knows their preferences, she pours coffee in any cup that's pushed toward the edge. She nears the end of the counter. "How about you, Kevin?" she asks.

"Yes, please do. I need it this morning."

"The hard stuff it is."

She empties the pot into his mug and sets it on the counter. "I don't recall seeing you looking so rough. Bad night?"

"Yeah, another all-nighter at work."

Gesturing to the white coat draped over the empty chair next to him, she says, "Remind me again, what kind of doctor are you?"

"Oh, I'm not a doctor."

"Sorry about that. I thought…"

Kevin interrupts, "No apologies. I get that all the time." He slides his ring back onto its proper finger and runs his hands through his messy hair. He says, "It must be my distinguished salt-and-pepper."

Loretta chuckles, "Yeah, that must be it."

She turns to walk away and Kevin pulls her back with a question that's intended to keep her attention. "Say, Loretta, give me an update on your boy. What's the latest?"

With enthusiasm, she replies, "Oh, my JT's having a great senior season. He leads the conference in nearly every stat. We've got a big local invitational tournament this weekend, then the state tourney just around the corner."

"Has he decided yet?"

She answers, "We're still weighing the options. He can't enter the NBA draft until he's at least nineteen years old and one year out of high school – some dumb rule."

"What about LeBron and Kobe – how'd they go straight in?"

"That was way before the rule change in 2006."

Kevin admitted, "I had no idea."

"Yeah, I'm learning as I go. I always thought James would handle this stuff when the time came. But, here we are, so I'm doing the best that I can."

"So, what until then," he asked.

Loretta leans over the counter, closer to Kevin, as if she's about to share a family secret. She begins bragging, "It depends who you ask. He says he wants to go to college to play ball; he keeps talking about Kentucky. But, I want him to go overseas for a year or two, then come back for the draft."

"Overseas?"

"Yeah, the Euroleague," Loretta proudly explains. "I've been talking to an international agent. See, JT can't, and won't, have contact with professional agents because it would make him ineligible for college ball. But, if he goes over there he could get paid. It ain't NBA money but we really need him to get paid." Her plan is revealed.

Kevin replies, "I get it."

"Either way, we need to commit soon."

The diner manager, an oversized grump, slides up next to Loretta and loudly clears his throat in a not-so-subtle way of interrupting. "Pardon me, but I hope your doctor friend here doesn't mind if you get back to your tables. You've got food in the window."

Loretta smugly replies, "I believe our consultation is just about over." With that, the boss man walks away.

Kevin laughs at the awkwardness and says, "That's okay, I've got to get going anyway. I've got some sleep to catch." He stands and gathers up his belongings. Kevin reaches into his pocket and peels off a twenty-dollar bill from his money clip. He smoothly places it on the counter and walks away. With a wave he says, "Have a great day, Lo!"

Swiping the cash from the counter, she replies, "I love it when you sit at my counter."

A few hours pass and Loretta is nearing the end of her six-hour shift. She's already making plans in her head for how she'll execute her routine motherly duties that night. While sneaking a peak at the clock near the front door, she notices Trina Kelley, her co-worker, relief and dear friend strolling across the parking lot. As Trina sluggishly makes her way into the diner, she stops briefly to chat with the manager. Loretta hustles over to meet her near the time clock, their gossip station.

Loretta greets her, "Hey girl, how's your day been?"

Normally, Trina is a bubbly redhead, rarely at a loss for words. However, today, there is no immediate reply from her.

"The tips have been…". Loretta stops to notice Trina's red-rimmed eyes; it's obvious that she has been crying. She inquires, "What's wrong, dear? Are you okay?"

"Not really," Trina replied. I hate to ask this of you but is there any way you can cover my shift tonight?"

"I really can't. We're still a one car family and JT needs to be picked up from school."

"You know I wouldn't ask if it weren't important. It's Bryan."

Loretta said, "Oh, how's he doing?"

"We had an appointment this morning." Trina becomes tearful again. "It's end stage now."

Loretta offers Trina a comforting hug, "I'm really sorry, Honey." She holds her friend closely, allowing her to express her emotions as she considers the value of her time. "I'll tell you what I'll do. Let me go pick up JT and drop him at home with his little brother. Then, I'll come back and work your shift."

Trina pulls herself away from Loretta's hug and looks her in the eye. "Would you really do that for me?"

"Hell, I could use the money too," Loretta quips.

"You're such a doll, I owe you one."

Loretta jokingly responds, "Really, just one?"

"I know, I know."

Loretta waves off her own facetiousness. "You know, we need to plan another dinner. Some much-needed girl time."

Trina briefly stares off into space and tries to imagine that scenario, then reality brings her back. She shakes her head, declining the invitation. "I'd be worried about him the whole time."

"Well, the offer stands." Loretta, then, nods her head to the side in the general direction of their manager, who's working the register. "Did you clear it with Tubby?"

Trina replies, "Yeah, as I was walking in. He said it was up to you since you were the one working the double."

"Okay then, I'll head out of here and get back as soon as I can," Loretta said. "Keep your chin up, girl. The Lord has a plan for us all, don't forget that."

CHAPTER 3

Soft music and the scent of lavender fills the air of the candle-lit bedroom. There's just enough light to make out photos of Kevin and Sherry Mills on the bedside table. An open bottle of wine and two half-empty glasses sit on the same table; consumption was interrupted by passion.

A man, with familiar graying hair, is laying on top of a woman. Her face is hidden, but her flowing blonde hair can be seen fanning out on the surface of the bed. Silky sheets cover their bodies as they are engaged in passionate lovemaking. His rhythmic motion is broken so to apply soft kisses to her neck. This movement reveals the face of Sherry Mills.

She reaches up and grabs hold of his hair, firmly directing him back to her mouth. They kiss with desire and passion. Their movements increase with intensity until a mutual climax occurs. The man rolls over, off of Sherry, to reveal his face; the face of a stranger.

Kevin Mills bolts upright in bed, like an old jack-in-the-box clown; sweat beading up on his forehead, breathing heavily. He rubs his eyes and quickly scans the bedroom –

he's alone. He collapses back into his pillows and stares straight up at the ceiling. "What the hell was that," he asks aloud as he rolls over toward the nightstand and reaches for his phone.

Sherry is finishing up her Friday work day. As she exits the building of her last appointment, she hears the familiar ring tone indicating a text message from her husband. She digs through her gigantic purse to find her phone. Mixed emotions flood her mind as she reads the message from Kevin: "CAN WE PLEASE TALK? I MISS MY WIFE!"

The message stops her in her tracks and Sherry says, softly to herself, "I miss you too." Tucking her phone away, she proceeds through the parking lot to her car. Once situated in the soft leather seat of her high-end SUV, she pulls out her phone and reads the message again. Her eyes soften as she contemplates the call, then she nervously dials his number.

The ringing phone startles Kevin and he sits straight up in bed. He can't help but smile ear-to-ear when he sees his wife's name displayed on the screen. The joy in his voice equals the joy in heart as he exuberantly answers the call, "Hey babe! Thanks for calling."

In a reserved tone, she replies, "Hi, Kev. How you doing?"

"Miserable, and you?"

"I've been better."

34

"Well, then, come on home and let's fix this."

Sherry replies, "I can't, not until there are real changes. You know how I feel."

"Can we at least get together soon to talk?" Recalling his dream, he says, "This is, literally, haunting me!"

"When? You never had time before." She sneaks in a low blow.

"Now? I'm at home."

She replies, "I can't right now. I'm going out of town with my Mom and sister this weekend, we're leaving tonight." Sherry throws in another jab, "Did you see the sonogram?"

Kevin, fleetingly, drops the phone to his lap and tilts his head back with frustration. Careful not to get sucked into another fight, he forces a fake grin and presses the phone back to his face. He continues, "Yeah, great for them. But can we focus on us right now?"

"Sorry, I couldn't help myself," she said.

"Listen, I'm on call on Monday, but hopefully it's quiet. Let's shoot for the afternoon."

"That'll work for me," she agreed. "I need to get going. Goodbye Kevin."

"Okay, I love..." Kevin's heart-felt words get interrupted by a dial tone. The call ends as unexpectedly as it arrived.

He lays his head back down on the fluffy pillows of the relatively empty king-sized bed and closes his eyes. Slowly, he rolls over onto his side clutching his phone as he prepares to resume his sleep. A smile crosses his face as he focuses on the picture of Sherry on the bedside table. He says softly, "Monday it is."

CHAPTER 4

The bright sun peaks around the billowing clouds that are scattered across the afternoon sky. The air is brisk, but the sun is warm; usual for a late-winter day in St. Louis. The Arch, a landmark known as the Gateway to the West, towers over the city and is visible from the steps of Central City High School. She is a three-story school house built decades ago. Her age is showing by the condition of the grounds and disrepair of the brick and mortar. The school, once brimming with young minds, has suffered from what politicians refer to as urban sprawl. Enrollment is down and continues to decline as city-dwelling families have moved – some say escaped – from the city to suburbia; the surrounding counties. The neighborhood is, let's just say, less than a desirable place to live.

In most high schools, just about anywhere, Friday afternoons are electric; the energy is palpable for the upcoming weekend. It brings a break from the books and the rigors of schoolwork. It's a chance for the kids to relax and enjoy their youth. This Friday was no different at Loretta's son's high school, even more so. A tournament weekend for the Central City High School Greyhounds' varsity basketball team always brings added life to those hallways.

Eighteen disinterested students are scattered about a half-empty classroom. Ms. Holland, weary from her long week of shaping young minds, stands at the front of the class trying to capture the remaining shreds of attention the kids have as they anticipate that final bell. She glances at the digital clock on the wall, it reads 2:55. She announces to the class, "Well, that's all for today. Be sure to review your notes this weekend. You never know, there just might be a pop quiz on Monday."

Moans and groans erupt from the students.

"Good, then that means you heard me." The teacher continues, "Oh yeah, and for those of you planning to attend the basketball games this weekend to cheer on our Greyhounds, be safe and have fun. I'll see you there."

The school bell rings loudly, announcing the end of the day. Once lethargic as a bed of sloths, the students jump to their collective feet and herd themselves toward the door and out into the hallway with a newly found enthusiasm that only a Friday afternoon can bring.

Mixed in with the swarm of young humanity is James Thomas Stone. He is the senior captain and two-time High School All-American basketball player that all the kids admire and opponents fear. He is, quite literally, the big man on campus. JT, as everyone calls him, glides through the hallways standing a whole head (a shaved head at that) and shoulders above the other students. He possesses an athletic build beyond that of his eighteen years. Over the noise of the bustling hallway, words of praise and well-wishes for JT fill the air, along with the occasional high-five for anyone that can manage the jump.

"GO, JT!"

"GOOD LUCK THIS WEEKEND!"

"BRING US HOME ANOTHER CHAMPIONSHIP, JT!"

He's their hero and he can't help but smile with pride. He loves the attention and can surely handle the pressure.

Loretta is sitting in their old, beat-up family car on a side street next to the school. It's the pre-arranged pick up spot because she hates getting stuck in the bus traffic. JT emerges from the school building with a small entourage of buddies and they playfully make their way toward the car, tossing the ever-present basketball between them. Once the group is within ear-shot, Loretta impatiently leans across the front seat and cranks down the window. She yells out, "JT, quit fussing with them boys. We gotta get going."

JT opens the passenger door and tosses his backpack onto the floor of the car. He manages to cram himself into the tight quarters and slams the door shut. He says, "We need an SUV, bad."

Loretta replies, "Yeah, it's on the list, right behind that

trip to Hawaii."

"Huh, for real, Mom?"

"No, don't be silly boy. We can't afford that." Loretta pulls the car onto the busy street and begins to navigate her way toward home. She turns to him and asks, "How was school today?"

"It was alright, same old stuff really. Except, lots of talk about the tournament this weekend."

"You ready?"

His cocky reply was, "I was born ready."

"Of course, you were. I was there, remember?"

A bit of a silent pause takes over the car as JT reaches for the stereo knob. "Hey Ma, what do you think about me getting a tattoo?"

Surprised, she responds, "A WHAT?"

JT extends his right arm out in front of him, the span easily reaches the windshield of the relatively tiny compartment. He explains, "I'm thinking like 3-1-4 across my shooting arm with a b-ball behind it, with a bunch of shadowing. Gotta represent The Lou."

Loretta fires back, "And who's paying for that?"

"Well…"

She interrupts, "Boy, you know I can't even afford that iPhone you keep asking for."

"All my buddies have them."

40

"What, the phone or the tattoo?"

In a disappointed tone, he replies, "Both."

Loretta shakes her head in disagreement. "Keep your eye on the prize and you'll have anything you want."

JT lowers his gaze out the window at the passing city sidewalk. He begins to daydream about his future and his past; a future free from these petty issues and the past wishes his Father secretly shared with him regarding his future.

James was a proud father and especially proud of the accomplishments of his eldest son. He did everything he could to attend each of JT's games, particularly the tournaments – those were his favorite because of the excitement of the players, coaches and fans and the immediate gratification that came from winning the title.

James worked hard to provide JT with the opportunities to develop his game to the level it has attained. But his efforts were not with the sole intent of his son making it the NBA. James wanted JT to go to college to play ball and earn his degree. Several reasons motivated this; first of all, no one in James' family ever went to college and he wanted that for his boys more than anything. Secondly, James was a Division One College Basketball fanatic. He more than just followed the teams and the different conferences, he

41

followed the players and the recruitment process too. He wanted to learn everything he could so he could be the expert when his son needed him the most – to help guide decisions regarding what school and which basketball program was the best fit for his son.

JT's daydreams took him back to a particular moment just over three years ago. During his Freshman year, JT was brought up to play on the Varsity Basketball Team at Central City High School. This was the crowning moment for his father, it was then that JT realized the extreme pride his father felt for his success but also for the fact that his son was going to achieve the dreams that he had envisioned for him; having the talent to play College Basketball.

During the NCAA Division One Basketball Tournament that year, late March of 2011, James shared his secret and deep desires with JT for him to play college ball. They didn't know where yet, and that didn't matter at the moment. He also shared with JT his secret selfish dream of sitting in the stands during a Final Four Championship game and having the TV cameras on him as the announcers described him as the "Father of a collegiate star."

These were secret dreams because James knew that Loretta had other hopes for JT, she had her own dreams of being the Mother of an NBA star.

Like most parents, they shared a desire of success for

their children; they just disagreed on the timeframe and the route it would take.

JT understood the importance of this to his Dad and decided during that two-week period in the Spring of 2011 that he was going to make sure that he made his Dad proud and fulfilled his dream for his son to play Division One Basketball, and more importantly, to obtain a college education.

He returns to the conversation with a more serious tone and asks, "Ma, do you really think I've got the game for the Euroleague right now?"

Loretta responds, "Hell yes! I've been saying this all along. Everybody thinks so - except you."

"Yeah, you've been pushing this straight-to-the-pros thing since the Sports Illustrated article last season. I wish they hadn't gotten that in your head."

"Well, I wish it had gotten into yours," she fires back. "Apparently, a team over there thinks so too. Mr. Murphy says there's talk of six-figures for a two-year deal."

"Ma, if you keep talking to that agent I could lose my eligibility for college ball."

"That's why you're not and I am, I'm dealing with it," she replies.

JT fires back, "Yeah, you're dealing with it, but only considering what you want. What about what I want?"

Without realizing it, Loretta is speeding and swerving around on the busy city streets. Another awkward pause as the tension in the car mounts. It's not the first time they've had this argument and it gets exponentially maddening for Loretta each time. "Listen JT, you know our situation and you know what you've got; a winning lottery ticket. You're gifted, everybody says so. What's wrong with cashing in that ticket now?"

"But Ma, it's my ticket to cash when I'm ready to cash it."

Becoming increasingly impatient with the conversation, she says, "It's your game baby. No one's taking that away from you. But, don't for one second, fool yourself into believing that this doesn't affect a lot of people. This is OUR ticket; yours, Mikey's, mine. We're all in this together. I've earned this too with all the sacrificing that I've had to make along the way."

JT silently gazes out the window and considers his Mother's position as their car rolls up to a red light. He spots a group of teen-aged boys loitering on the opposite corner. Just then, another car pulls up for what appears to be an illegal transaction of sorts, not a rare sight in their neighborhood.

Loretta continues as her voice begins to crack with emotion, "Don't you want to get out of this neighborhood, out of that nasty apartment we live in, this janked-up car, this life?"

"Of course, I do! But, I also want to do what's best for me. Ever since Dad died, I've had to step up and be the man of the house. I'm trying to take care of Mikey when you're on the job, keeping my grades up and working on my game."

"And?"

JT gestures to the gang on the street corner, "That could easily be me over there, but it ain't."

"Boy, don't give me that crap," Loretta responds. She guns the car off the line as the stop light turns green like she's in a drag race.

"Ma, I want to make a decision for myself for a change. I just want to be a kid while I can."

Loretta's impatience is morphing into frustration. "Nobody is saying that you can't make this decision. You just need to consider *everyone* involved when you make it."

"Whatever," he says defiantly.

Loretta turns another corner.

Once again, JT finds himself stuck in the middle. It's a tough choice for such a young man to have to make; support his family or honor his dead Father's dreams. The moment has arrived for him, it's time to share his true feelings. In a softer tone, an attempt to de-escalate the situation, he says, "I guess what I'm trying to say is that I think I want to go play college ball at Kentucky. I really like what they've offered. I want to experience college life. I want to be in that big tournament, hopefully, the Final Four, maybe win a National Championship along the way."

Loretta takes a final turn and pulls up to their dilapidated housing unit on the city's north side. She slams the car into park.

Reflecting again on his Father's wishes, he adds, "Besides, a college education could secure a future for us beyond basketball, not just a payday."

Taken aback, Loretta mumbles softly so only she can hear, "Man, it's hard to argue with someone smarter than you." Louder now, for JT to hear, she declares, "We'll talk about this later."

JT opens the car door and manages to wrestle one of his lengthy lower extremities out of the door.

"Is Stevie's Momma still picking you up in the morning?"

"Yup," he replied.

"Good. Make sure your brother eats dinner too and you're both in bed early. We've got a crazy-busy weekend ahead."

The thought of food perks him up. Eating takes a close

46

second to sleep on JT's list of favorite pastimes. "What's for dinner," he asks in a hopeful voice.

"There's a pizza in the freezer. Chips are in the pantry on the top shelf. I had to hide them from Mikey."

"Frozen pizza? Ma, the coach said to have a good meal tonight."

"Boy, that is a good meal. It ain't Ramen," she jokes. "Listen, I've got to get back to the diner. I'll be home after you boys are in bed."

JT snatches his backpack from the floorboard and manages to lumber the rest of his big frame out of the little car. He replies, "Fine, I'll see you at the game." Fairly disgusted with that entire conversation, JT slams the door shut just as his mom mutters, "Love you." He was oblivious to it.

Loretta, clearly distraught, pulls away from the curb. A scowl appears on her face as she realizes that her master plan may be unraveling.

CHAPTER 5

Kevin Mills guides his import into the nearly empty parking lot of the Missouri Donor Network office building and locates some prime real estate in the front row. Saturdays are not usual office days and casual when necessary. Jeans, a North Face jacket and his customary Cardinals cap are appropriate attire on this day.

He stopped off at his favorite little bagel shop on his way in for his staple; an everything, toasted, with Taylor ham and a thick smear of cream cheese with chopped green olives – "an acquired taste," he explains to anyone that turns up their nose at it. With a small brown bag containing his breakfast treat in one hand, his leather messenger bag slung over his left shoulder and a steaming hot cup of coffee stinging the fingers on his other hand, he approaches the front door to his building. Kevin pauses to place the coffee cup down and reaches for the front door. Just as he does, the door swings wide open. Amy Mann, a spirited young female employee springs through the door to greet him. "Hey, Mr. Mills, I saw you pull in and figured you could use a hand. What brings you in on a Saturday morning?"

"Good morning to you, Amy. Thanks for the assist." As he passes through the doorway he asks, "How's the Comm Center this morning?"

She replies, "Actually, it's a little quiet. Strange for a Saturday. Say, I don't have you as being on call today, what gives?"

Not feeling the need to share his life's problems with the office staff, Kevin spews out a generic response, "I came in to work on some charts. Thought I'd get a jump on the day."

Their office building is fairly new. The modern state-of-the-art facility was constructed just three years ago, from the ground up. MDN has always been an innovative leader in the field of Organ Procurement. With visionary leadership and the exceptional clinical staff that they've recruited, this organization has broken down barriers that have existed since organ transplantation and procurement began in the mid 1950's.

MDN was the first Organ Procurement Organization in the country to purchase, customize and utilize their own airplane for donor and organ transportation. They were also the first OPO to build on-site clinical facilities for donor management and operating room suites for organ and tissue procurement surgeries outside of the hospital setting.

This new building houses the first cardiac catheterization lab of its kind, used exclusively for donor organ assessments. Kevin Mills played a major role in each of these innovative milestones; his value to this organization is immeasurable.

Once they are both inside the vestibule, Amy walks toward the glass enclosure that bears the etching, COMMUNICATIONS CENTER. It's a darkened room, filled with computer terminals, closed circuit monitors and switchboards; it's the brain room of the operation. All referrals for organ and tissue donation go through that room and the several highly-trained staff that manage it.

Kevin says, "I'll probably only be here for the morning. Thanks again for your help."

"No worries. Don't work too hard."

He laughs at his reply, "That's the plan."

Kevin casually makes his way through the expansive, open floor plan to his cubicle. His little eight-by-eight workspace is decorated with St. Louis Cardinals and St. Louis Blues paraphernalia. The nameplate on the outer wall reads, "KEVIN MILLS, RN, BSN, CCRN, CPTC," "ORGAN PROCUREMENT COORDINATOR". Several certifications, awards and plaques cover the three-quarter walls. He is proud of his accomplishments, as he should be. In addition to his Bachelor's Degree in Nursing, Kevin has gone on to advanced achievements in the field of nursing. He holds two national certifications, one in Critical Care

Nursing and one in Organ Procurement. These are two extremely difficult tests used to separate the best from the rest, in each of the specialties - to hold Certification in both speaks volumes to Kevin's intelligence, dedication and commitment to his field.

As he sets his bag on his desk he notices the open door and lighted office of his boss, Gary Jennings. He quietly says to himself, "What are the odds of that?" With coffee cup in hand, Kevin begins to walk along the perimeter of the room, toward the office of his close friend. Upon his arrival, Kevin raps his knuckles on the door frame of the open office door.

Gary looks up from his desk to see his buddy standing there. Surprised, he says, "Hey, what's up, Kevin? What are you doing here?"

"You know me, boss - Mr. Dedication."

"You want to know the craziest thing? I was going to call you to see about grabbing some lunch today. We need to catch up."

"Well, we can certainly do that, I've got nothing else going on."

Gary, sensing the sarcasm in Kevin's voice and knowing the situation on the home front, asks, "Sherry's still gone?"

"Yeah, no bueno at home. Do you mind if I come in?"

"Hell no, get in here."

They have known each other since the early years of their careers. They were two of just a handful of male nurses on the ICU, so their bond was forged out of survival. It can be tough as a young man working in a field predominately made up of women. Gary had been in the ICU for five years before Kevin came along as the newbie on the unit. He noticed the talent and intelligence early on and took Kevin in, under his wing. He showed him the ropes and taught him things that you never learn in school about being a Critical Care Nurse.

Two years after Kevin joined the ICU, Gary was recruited by MDN. In a way, he was paving the career path that Kevin is now traveling. When Kevin was recruited by MDN, it was Gary that orchestrated that acquisition. He knew the good that Kevin would be able to do for his organization and the people they serve.

In addition to their work, they have many other things in common. Their mutual love, obsession really, for St. Louis sports, especially Cardinals Baseball. They would often take in the Thursday, businessman special, day games at Busch Stadium. But, a truer sign of their friendship is the rare fact that they've attended three Cardinals World Series games together. Only a handful of buddies can brag about that.

They were the best of friends. So, it was common for

them to confide in one another both professionally and personally. Gary has been there throughout this long debate Kevin and Sherry have been having about their family issue; from the sidelines, of course. But, the conversation Kevin was about to have with Gary drew the two perspectives together, for the first time.

Kevin enters Gary's office and quietly takes a seat on the couch across from his desk. In a sullen tone, Kevin begins, "I've just got a bad feeling. I think there might be someone else."

Gary pauses and takes a look out the office window, unsure if he should divulge the secret. "There's something I need to tell you. I wasn't sure-"

"What," Kevin interrupts.

"It's probably nothing."

Kevin insists, "What it is?"

"It's Sherry. I saw her at a restaurant last Wednesday afternoon, with a guy."

In an instinctive effort to defend her, he says, "So what, she takes doctors to lunch all the time."

Gary drops the bomb, "Yeah, but do they hold hands?"

Kevin leans back into the couch, drops his head and recalls the letter. He whispers the revelation to himself, "Options. Now I get it."

Straining to hear what Kevin just said, Gary says,

"What?"

Kevin re-engages in the conversation, "Nothing. I'm sure it's nothing. She wouldn't do that to me." His voice may sound convincing, but his head and heart can't help but ponder the possibilities.

"I'm sorry, buddy. Maybe she's just trying to get your attention."

Kevin replies, "Well, she's got it." He searches for anything to change the uncomfortable subject. He, then, continues, "No, nothing has changed. Sherry is still at her parent's house. We're supposed to be getting together on Monday to talk."

"That's a good thing, right?"

"Well, that depends on what side of the fence you're on." Kevin sits forward in his seat, ready to drop a bomb of his own. "Brace yourself - she's asking me to quit MDN."

"What, you quit transplant?"

The thought of it has Kevin choking on his words. "She's serious this time, she's gonna divorce me."

Recognizing that his friend is hurting, Gary stands up and walks around his desk and sits next to Kevin on the couch. He places his hand on Kevin's shoulder and says, "We've been friends for a long damn time. I'm talking to you as your buddy now, not your boss. What do you want to do?"

Kevin considers his question carefully, then confesses, "She's my everything."

"Then, it seems simple to me, she needs to know that. So, if it means you can't be a procurement coordinator then that's what needs to happen."

Kevin sits back on the couch again and shakes his head in agreement. "Wow, this isn't the response I expected from you. You're really okay with me quitting?"

Gary stands up and leisurely takes his seat back behind his desk. "Now that I'm back in this chair, hell no I'm not okay with you leaving. Are you crazy?"

Kevin launches himself back upright and says, "Now, I'm really confused."

"You're far too valuable to this organization to just let you walk away, even if it is for a good reason." Gary continues, "Listen, buddy, I told you that I was working on something for you."

"Yeah, but you said it was a long shot. Did it actually come through?"

"Yup, I found out late yesterday afternoon. You're the new Manager of Clinical Procurement, if you want it."

Kevin sits with his mouth open, in shock.

Gary continues, "You'll report to me and be in charge of the organ procurement team."

Kevin finally manages to speak, "That's amazing!" He

pauses to consider the other perks, then continues, "Wait, no more call?"

"Not unless you want to take some. It's not required of the leadership team," Gary explains.

"I don't know what to say."

"Say yes and we'll make the announcement at Tuesday's staff meeting. It will be effective on Wednesday."

"YES, HELL YES!" Kevin looks around the cluttered office, trying to absorb the news. "Wow, Monday will be my last day of call? That's unbelievable."

"You've earned this, Kevin. It's not a gift."

"I appreciate it, I really do."

Kevin stands and approaches Gary, hand extended. The handshake becomes a bear-hug. "Sherry's gonna love this. I'll tell her on Monday."

Breaking their "bro-mantic" embrace, Gary asks, "What are you going to do about her and this guy I saw her with?"

Kevin takes a moment to ponder that question. "I'll confront her with it and hope that she can be honest with me."

"Be careful what you hope for, Kev. You just might get it."

CHAPTER 6

The St. Louis High School Invitational Basketball Tournament is an annual viewing of what the area has to offer colleges in the way of Prep School basketball talent. Recruiters from all the top collegiate programs make this yearly trek to the Midwest on this February weekend. It's still early enough in the season to entice those scholar-athletes who are planning on attending college but haven't yet committed to that one school that's best for them.

What made this year's tournament extra special was the number of scouts in attendance, twice as many as ever before. JT Stone was the reason, they all want his talent. With about six weeks left in the 2014 campaign, the number one high school player in the country has yet to commit to any one institution. Rumor and speculation on the part of sports media have him going to The University of Kentucky, the so-called breeding ground for the NBA. But, what none of them knew were the plans that Loretta had for JT's future. Nonetheless, they all had a shot as long as no commitment papers were signed.

All of these men, with their various credentials and stacks of statistics, were crammed into a section of designated bleacher seats on the North side of the gym, the home team side. Among them, sits a special guest of Loretta Stone. He stands out from the rest; perhaps it's the custom Italian suit that screams "money". His name is Mr. William Murphy. He's there to keep track of JT's future, on Loretta's behalf, and if possible find some time to secretly meet with him. Murphy's sole job is to execute Loretta's plan; to convince JT to take the money and run away to Europe. He stands to benefit financially as well as JT's formal representative, a selfish little perk.

The weekend tournament went pretty much as predicted with the two top-ranked teams in the state meeting in the final on Sunday afternoon. The home team Trinity Prep Titans are facing JT Stone and the Central City Greyhounds. What no one correctly predicted was the score at halftime. The Greyhounds found themselves down by four points; The Titans – 40 and The Greyhounds - 36.

Inside the squalid Visitor's locker room, sit twelve wearied players; some physically, all emotionally. They sit in silence, reflecting on the first-half and waiting for the verbal lashing they've got coming. The finishing five are still trying to catch their breath, dripping with sweat.

Among them is their star-player, JT Stone. Despite the score, he portrays a confidence that the other players don't seem to have. The athletic trainer is tending to the knee of a wounded warrior on the training table as Coach Duane

Miller and his assistants emerge from behind the bank of lockers to address the team.

Coach Miller was never one to scream or yell at his players, but his voice is easily heard that afternoon. "Okay, that was not what I was expecting from the top-ranked team in the state. You are better than that, we are better than that!"

He begins pacing the floor between the benches that his boys occupy. "We're down by four and now we're also down a starter." The Coach points over in the direction of the injured Greyhound, and says, "Trey's out". Ramping up his tone, Coach Miller continues, "Guys, this tournament is the showcase of Missouri High School Basketball. We are the best team here, but that half doesn't reflect that!" The Coach pauses to catch his breath, then continues his rant, "Last year's loss to these guys was heartbreaking. Don't let that happen again. I guarantee that it'll hurt more this year because we are graduating four of our five starters."

The boys look around the room, imagining what a different scene next year will be for each of them. JT's vision of the future, however, is extremely different.

"The State Tournament starts in three weeks. Let's use this as a springboard to that. Let's fight our way to the top," Coach Miller exclaims, trying to get his guys fired up.

"Gentlemen, come in closer." The players creep in slowly and huddle around their mentor. "I'm not gonna talk

X's and O's; you guys know how to execute our game. I want to talk to you about something else now." The Coach takes a moment to survey the eyes of his young men. He is speaking to them as a group, but is sending messages to them individually with his eye contact. He continues, "Twenty to thirty years from now, you may find yourself reflecting on your life. You'll be looking for those special moments that altered your life's direction one way or the other. When that happens, and I promise you that it will, I want you to have this day come to mind. There are college scouts out there. Prove to them who you are and what you're worth to them; create an opportunity for yourself. Men, make this day a defining moment in your life!"

Coach Miller pauses to allow his words to wash over the boys. Several of them give nods of approval while the others stare in admiration for their coach. "That's all I have, gentlemen. You've got three minutes until we take that floor. Talk it over."

JT, quickly, springs to his feet. The players admire their coach, but they love their leader. "Coach Miller is right! This is our time! Let's go out there and execute our game. If we play the best we can, no holding back, we can and we will come back and take this championship!"

The players begin to feel the building momentum in the room with each spoken word from their Captain. "I promise each of you that I'm gonna be a sniper out there. Stevie, own those damn boards! Dante, use that speed and those ball skills! If we all step up together, we will make this one of those moments!"

All the players jump to their feet with shouts of agreement, inspired by what they've just heard. They form a tight huddle around their leader. Locking arms, they begin to sway to the left and then to the right, in unison. A slow chant builds: "GREYHOUNDS, GREYHOUNDS, GREYHOUNDS!"

The half-time entertainment consisted of cheerleading routines from each of the schools. Not quite as enjoyable as the basketball action, but fun to watch in their own right. The energy in the standing room only gymnasium is palpable now as the home court fans, donning their crimson and white colors, are on their feet cheering when their team begins the second half warm-up.

The Visitor's locker room doors are pushed open by two security guards. Lead by Coach Miller and JT Stone, the Greyhound players take the court. As they do, their fans jump to their collective feet to welcome them back to the floor.

Half-way up the visiting team bleachers, with a great vantage point, sits Loretta Stone. She is swimming in one of JT's jerseys, draped over a hoodie. Sitting next to Loretta is her fancy, well-kept, younger sister, Tanya Peterson. She married into some money, which has always been a bone of contention between the sisters. Loretta's not really a jealous person; envious is the proper word for it. She has eternally had to work hard for what's hers and has had more than her fair share of challenges in her life. However, Tanya has been a big help to her sister in the recent years, since James' untimely death. She has been supportive, both emotionally and financially, when needed, to make sure her sister and nephews didn't fall between the cracks.

Smashed between the sisters is Loretta's youngest boy, Mikey. At nine years of age, he's easily JT's biggest fan. He looks up to him in many ways, aside from the obvious. With no real father figure, except for his big brother, Mikey has struggled at times with behavior issues, especially at school. Loretta has done her best to be everything that a young, impressionable boy needs, but she can only do so much. Her hope is that this master plan will help take care of these issues before they manifest into something she can't control. So much rides on her design.

Loretta leans into Tanya and says, "Let's hope this half is better than that last one. They look more energized at least."

"Maybe that coach put the fear of God in them," Tanya said.

"Or, maybe his boot!"

Both women laugh as the horn blasts through the noise of the crowd, signaling the impending start of the second half.

Straining on his tip-toes, looking toward the group of scouts, Mikey asks, "Hey Ma, wasn't that guy at our house before? That one too?"

"Yeah, there's a bunch of them over there."

Tanya says, "You think they're all here to see JT?"

Loretta responds proudly, "You've got that right, sister! We've been calling them The Clipboard Kings because they think they control our destiny." Shaking her head back and forth in disagreement, Loretta smugly says, "Nope, I'm running this Queendom."

Tanya forces an awkward laugh, and says, "Yeah you are!"

As if on cue, Mikey begins pulling on Loretta's jersey. He's not one for cordial interruptions. He says, "Mommy, can I have some money to get a Coke?"

Loretta shoots him a dirty look as she roots through her purse. She pulls some loose change and says, "Here's a dollar, or close to it. I had to work real hard for that."

"But that's not gonna be enough."

"You'll have to make it work. I need my dollar bills."

Tanya reaches in her purse, removes her designer wallet, pulls out a five spot and hands it over. "Wow, thanks

65

Auntie Tanya," Mikey shouted.

"Where's my thank you, boy? And, my change," Loretta fires back as Mikey works his way down the bleachers and disappears into the crowd.

There is fierce action up and down the court with cheerful eruptions from the crowd. JT Stone is controlling this half of the game with fancy passing, three pointers and an occasional slam dunk. "It's a tight game. At least they are looking better this half," Tanya comments. She gestures to the recruiter's section and nudges Loretta's arm, "Are those guys really here just to see JT?"

"Well, I'm sure it's not all about him. But, I do recognize most of them from meetings at our apartment. The guy I care about most is on the far end. That's William Murphy, the sports agent I told you about," Loretta replied.

"Oh, girl, he is handsome."

Loretta playfully slaps Tanya's arm, "Oh, don't be silly. He ain't my type."

Tanya laughs off her comment and asks, "He's the Euroleague guy, right?"

"Yup, he's gonna make that happen for us."

Tanya rolls her eyes a bit and says, "Yeah, I know what you want - that payday! But what about Kentucky?"

Loretta quickly shakes her head in denial and responds, "No. He needs to go overseas for a couple of years, then

66

come back and enter the NBA draft." She confidently continues, "If his Daddy was alive, he'd say the same thing." Of course, Loretta was aware of her dearly-departed husband's dreams of college for his sons and an NCAA basketball career for JT. They used to argue about JT's path privately, but never in front of the children. Her current plan and needs take priority now that he's gone; as she sees it, respectfully, James' dreams for JT's future won't pay her current bills.

Tanya cautiously probes a bit further, asking, "Lo, are you sure you want to bring James into this? Don't you think he'd be proud either way? Besides, I think JT actually wants to go to college. It's more than just basketball to him."

"Don't be silly. What boy with his talent doesn't dream of the NBA?" Loretta continues, "This may be our only chance at a future, a good one."

"But, isn't that your…"

Loretta scowls and points her finger at her younger sister, "Watch it!"

"Yeah, but…"

Loretta interrupts her again, "Look, you're my baby sister and I do love you, but you need to stay in your lane."

Tanya replies, "But, pushing your dreams onto him is bound to blow up in your face."

"Look, Tanya, you've got a different life than I do and

I'm happy for you. You've got a good job and a nice man that takes care of things for you. I don't have that at the moment. My struggles are real!"

The discomfort of the topic is evident on their faces and their attention returns to the game action. In an effort to change the subject, Loretta says, "You know, JT asked me for a tattoo a couple days ago. I swear that boy thinks I print money in the basement."

"Girl, you don't have a basement."

Playfully laughing together, Loretta says, "Exactly!"

The crowd is in a frenzy of excitement as the championship game is coming down to the wire. There have been three different lead changes and the Greyhounds have managed to fight their way back. They are still two points down with thirty-two seconds left in regulation.

JT and his boys are in a man-to-man defense, trying not to give up any more points. The Titans pass the ball around the arc, with precision, looking for a hole. JT manages to anticipate a pass and lunges forward to intercept with twenty seconds on the clock. With ball in hand, he sees the light and streaks down the court toward the unguarded net. As he effortlessly dribbles across the foul line, he leaps with Jordan-esque fashion, gliding through the air, and slams the ball into the hoop with a two-fisted spinning dunk to tie the game.

The Titans' crowd falls silent.

The Central City Greyhounds' fans are making up for it. The gym is filled with screams and cheers. JT glances over to his bench, as he heads back down court, to see his boys celebrating in amazement.

Coach Miller, all business, screams instructions from the sideline, "Press 'em! Press 'em!"

JT yells out, "Pick up your man! Mark up!"

The Greyhounds' players aggressively attack the inbound effort of the Titans. The ball is passed into their star player and he is immediately and intentionally fouled by Dante to stop the clock. This results in two free throws for the Titans' best shooter. On the other end of the court, the free-throws are made with ease giving the Titans a two-point lead with 00:10 left on the clock.

Coach Miller grabs the attention of the referee and yells, "Time out, ref!" The Greyhounds' players approach the sideline chairs with wobbly legs. Their collective effort this half is unmatched by any other the entire season - they have certainly left it all on the floor, as they say. Corralling the team in with his arms as he takes a knee, Coach Miller says, "Bring it in boys!" The floor players take seats on the chairs, along the sideline. The rest of the team members crowd in, tightly around, creating a cone of silence. The Coach begins, "You've done exactly what we talked about at the half.

You've fought back and put us in a position to win this game. We're ten seconds and one shot away from finishing this thing." He confidently looks at JT, "How ya feeling? You got one more left?"

"All day long, Coach. You get me that rock and it's over!"

Coach Miller reaches over and proudly rubs JT's sweaty bald head, looks at his wet hand then reaches for a towel. "We know they're gonna put two on JT, so that means we're gonna inbound with play number four. Got it?"

The players all stand with complete confidence and agreement, huddling around their coach. JT shouts above the crowd noise, "Hands in!" He pauses and stares directly into the eyes of his teammates and his coach, "Boys, if we play these last few seconds like they're our last, there's no way we can lose!"

The team begins to get fired up as arms reach in from all directions and collect in the middle of the tight circle. JT leads them, "One, two, three…"

"GREYHOUNDS!"

The stands erupt in ovation as both teams take the court like worn out gladiators arriving on the coliseum floor. They take their positions and, as predicted, the Titans put a double team on JT. The ref hands the ball off to Dante, the Greyhounds' All-Conference shooting guard, and he starts movement along the baseline. He's looking to inbound to Stevie Howard, JT's best buddy, who was left unattended as a result of the double team. Just as the play is designed, the ball is worked into Stevie. JT shakes loose of his shadows and streaks toward the half court line.

The crowd has begun the countdown.

Time slows to a snail's pace as the ball is released from Stevie in an overhand Manning-like pass directly into the path of the sprinting JT. He knocks the ball to the floor and dribbles to the three-point arc and pulls up for a jumper. As the ball leaves his fingertips the clock reaches 00:00. The ref raises both hands, indicating a three-point attempt as the defender's leap to block the shot is just shy.

The silence in the gym is deafening.

SWISH! Nothing but net!

The Greyhounds' bench empties onto the court and the celebration ensues as the scoreboard declares the winner: HOME 87, VISITORS 88.

The Greyhounds' fans join the on-court celebration. Mikey's small frame allows him to move freely among the trees of people to find his big brother. He hugs him tightly around the waist.

JT reaches down and grabs up his little brother and the two of them share a warm, loving embrace. With Mikey in his arms, the brothers scan the Greyhounds' fans that remain

71

in the bleachers and locate their mother. Loretta and Tanya are arm-in-arm, jumping in place with prideful exuberance. JT and Loretta share a long, warm gaze. It's a glimpse of their future and championships to come.

As the on-court celebration begins to settle, each of the Greyhounds players make their way into their locker room. A tournament-winning celebration is not new to this group, but this one has special meaning since they dropped this tournament last year. Once all inside, they try to contain their excitement so they can hear their coach commence his post-game talk.

Fighting back tears of joy, Coach Miller begins, "That had to be one of the gutsiest comeback wins I have ever seen, much less, been a part of. I've never been prouder! You guys really came together, just like you said you would." The coach turns to his assistant and motions for the game ball. He turns back to face his team. "This game ball is going to an individual. You led this team today, just as you have done all season. It's been my pleasure to be your coach for these past four years and to watch you grow and improve to be the player and fine young man that you are. This game ball goes to JT Stone."

All the players voice their unanimous and unopposed agreement. Coach Miller shoots a quick belly pass across the room to JT, who sure-hands the ball.

"Thanks, Coach. I can't tell you what it means to me to be a part of this team. I'll take this game ball from you, but I'm gonna give it right back to each of you guys. We did this together, today. All season we've battled, together. I can't thank you enough for the memories we've made. I will take them with me, wherever I go." JT lifts the ball over his head and the room erupts with cheers.

Coach Miller screams above the merriment, "Alright boys, enjoy this – you've earned it. But, grab quick showers and let's take this trophy and this party back to our school. I just got off the phone with Principal Melrose, they're going to have a welcome reception for us when we get there. Vans leave in thirty minutes."

Loud music begins to play from portable speakers that the team brought with them, for this very reason. The sounds of celebration fill the foul-smelling room as the team continues to revel in their victory.

CHAPTER 7

Madison Deveraux (nee DuPont) grew up in the Central West End, a higher-class section of town, which sits right on the edge of the downtown St. Louis city limits. It's outside the city proper just enough to lose that "big city feel." The streets are tree-lined and many of the neighborhoods are the private, gated kind that protects some of the highest priced homes in the city. Many of the mansions inside these exclusive areas were built in the late 1890's by wealthy business owners as part of the booming economic growth that took place at the turn of the century in St. Louis. These homes were constructed as "private places" for the wealthy to escape the hustle of the city, to what was then referred to as the country. The house Madison was raised in was one of these homes that were featured in the 1904 World's Fair Home Parade. It has been in her family for over a hundred years – old-money, as they say, and lots of it.

Madison met her husband, Theodore, while attending college at Washington University, in St. Louis. She was there to fulfill the wish of her dearly-departed grandmother and to collect her inheritance, which stipulated a college degree. Her major was "General Studies," so not to interfere with her other pursuit, finding the perfect husband. She was successful in both endeavors. Theo, as she likes to call him, was pre-law when they met. They both went on to graduate; him first and her one year later. Theo completed his Juris Doctorate two years later. They wed that summer, thus executing her Grandmother's secret plan to secure Madison's future, she never worked a day in her life.

Theo has spent his entire career living up to the pressure of marrying into an old-money family – will there ever be enough? His was a continuous endeavor to make sure that he proved himself worthy to Madison's family; it's what drives his success as a criminal defense attorney. His achievements and his notoriety, on a National level, come at a cost, however.

Sherry Mills is the eldest daughter of Theo and Madison Deveraux. She and her younger sister, Emily, spent most of their growing years under the direct supervision of their loving Mother and the staff that kept the hundred-year-old house running. Their Father was absent most of the time, even for many of the pivotal moments; birthdays, family vacations, sporting events, formal dances, etc. - but always there in spirit. He loved and provided for them, but he failed them in pursuit of his success. This was not lost on the young girls, particularly Sherry. Her dreams of marriage and family were completely different from her own personal experience; she longed for a husband that would be present and provide for her and their children. Marriage to a high-powered lawyer was never an option for her.

After the girls graduated from their private high schools, Madison elected to part ways with her old family home. She and Theo sold their Central West End mansion and relocated. They downsized, if you can call it that, to their four-thousand square foot, newly constructed "retirement" home. The staff was reduced to two. Theo scaled back his hours to a mere forty to fifty a week – all billable, of course. It was just the two of them now, as the girls' lives had taken off, each successful in their own rights.

When Sherry showed up on their doorstep a few weeks ago, she was of course welcomed with open arms. Madison was quietly and selfishly happy to have the company of her daughter. She was supportive and tried hard to allow Sherry to "have her space" without prying – just what Sherry needed and for which she asked.

Sherry and her Mother returned home from the airport in a rented limousine late on this Sunday afternoon. Theo was, of course, out of town prepping for a case in the Southern Missouri town of Springfield. After unpacking their newly acquired treasures and removing the feeling of travel from their bodies, the two ladies agreed to partake in their Sunday evening ritual; wine in the hearth room.

A warm fire roars in the oversized marble fireplace. Its heat and light creep into the dark and cozy room where Sherry and her mother are sharing a familiar glass of Pinot Grigio in a couple of finely upholstered, ample-sized, wingback chairs. The smell of pine fills the room along with the sound of low, soft music from the house-wide sound system.

"I forgot to ask you, how was your massage this morning," Madison inquired.

"Oh, it was wonderful. The hot stones were a nice touch. Thanks for suggesting it."

"I love our weekend trips away," Madison confessed. "I look forward to the next one even before the current one is over."

The girls have had a tradition; for years, they would take little weekend trips to cities that caught their interest. Usually, it was tourist-type destinations like Nashville, New York, Memphis, New Orleans or sometimes a quaint little town like South Haven, Michigan or Bay Head, New Jersey. These quarterly retreats were Madison's way of staying connected to her girls and their way of disconnecting from their busy lives. This most-recent trip was to Chicago for a weekend of shopping and a luxury hotel stay. It was Sherry's choice, as she felt like she needed the pampering. As usual, her Mother was eager to oblige – the tab always went to her.

The getaway was everything Sherry was hoping for, a much-needed respite from the troubles that she was having with Kevin. The one caveat was having to tolerate Emily's current state of pregnancy; one that Sherry is envious of and had been longing for, for years. The threesome survived the weekend, relationships intact.

"I know that our trips are usually more relaxing. I'm sorry if I brought the mood down for you at all," Sherry said.

"Not for me, but I got the sense that your sister felt slighted at times."

Sherry fired back, "Not everything needs to be about her, all the time. She's pregnant - we all get it."

Madison attempts to keep the conversation light by saying, "Now, I know, deep down, you're happy for your sister. But, we know you're struggling with your issues with Kevin."

Sherry takes a long slow drink from her glass of wine.

In her motherly-type tone, Madison continues, "Sherry, your Father and I will always support you and your decisions. But, that doesn't mean we necessarily have to agree with them."

"What does that mean, Mother?"

Madison tilts her glass back and finishes off the white wine. She reaches for the bottle in the chilling bucket between them and fills her glass, then she leans over and empties the bottle into Sherry's glass and divulges, "This wine has destroyed my filter."

Madison giggles while she pauses to consider crossing the line. Then she continues, "Oh, what the hell. Your sister is in a different situation than you. I would never say this in front of her and I'll deny it if it's brought up, but we're rooting for you and Kevin. He is a much better provider and, frankly, a better person than your brother-in-law, let's face it."

"Mom, that's not very-"

"I know it's not nice. But it's true. We love him too, but Kevin is a man of high integrity and has a heart of gold."

"Mom, that's not the issue at all," Sherry says.

"I know, it's the fact that you want a family. We get that, Sherry. But you need to step back and look at the big picture. You're both still young and there's time for that."

Sherry puts her hand up, motioning for her Mom to stop. She says, "Do you know that he nearly forgot my birthday last month? Yeah, that's right. It's just that I don't feel like a priority in his life. His job comes first, always."

"Okay, let's talk about that. He's doing something to help others. He saves lives for a living. Maybe you could be a little more understanding," Madison suggests.

Sherry takes another sip from her glass and stares deeply into the fire for a long minute. She asks her Mom, "Did I ever tell you why Kevin is so motivated when it comes to transplant?

"No, you haven't."

"He doesn't like to talk about it." Sherry explains, "His boyhood best friend died on the heart transplant list from an infection in his heart. He still gets upset to this day when he thinks about it."

"See, Sweetheart, he is a special man on a mission to do good for people, to make a difference. How noble a cause is that?"

A warm smile appears on Sherry's face, a warmth not induced by the fire's heat. She replies, "I know, Mother. He *is* special."

"Like I said, your Father and I support you, but we think you're making a big mistake by leaving him."

"Who said I was leaving him?"

"Hello? Where have you been sleeping these last couple of weeks? Sherry, I'm sorry, but I'm just going to say it; you need to go back home and be more supportive of him."

Sherry's gaze returns to the fire. She takes another long last drink from her glass and stares deeply into the dancing flames like a young child looking to her teacher for answers.

CHAPTER 8

The Stone Family often get treated like VIPs whenever it comes to anything basketball. For this reason, they are allowed to wait for JT near the school vans that are parked on the side of the gymnasium, away from the foot traffic of the departing fans. Their excitement continues, as evidenced by Mikey's inability to stand still while they wait for JT to make his post-game appearance. The side door of the building opens and JT appears, surrounded by teammates and cheerleaders. As the exuberant group approaches, Mikey runs over and jumps into the arms of his brother for a congratulatory hug.

"You're almost too big to be doing that, Bubba," JT says, jokingly to Mikey. "But, I'll take it any day." As they reach the family group, Mikey slides down JT's tall frame.

JT sets his bag on the ground, opens his arms and pulls his Mother in for a warm embrace. She says, aloud, "Son, that had to be one of your best games, ever."

"I haven't seen the numbers yet, but I think so too. It sure felt good."

Mikey asks, "Did you even miss a shot in the second half?"

"Um, no, I don't think I did. How about that, Buddy?"

Shaking his head in disbelief, "Awesome! That'll be me some day."

JT rubs Mikey's head and squeezes him close to his hip, "Keep up the hard work and don't let up, you'll get there."

Tanya reaches up and puts an arm around JT. With a half-hug she says, "Congrats! Winning the State Tourney is next, I guess. What a way to finish your high school career."

"Yup, that's our plan."

Loretta asks JT, "Did you see that Mr. Murphy is here?"

JT rolls his head and shrugs his shoulders, "Who?"

"Come on, you know who I'm talking about. He was looking for you after the game."

"No, I managed to avoid all of those guys, the media too, by sliding out that back door. I could go pro in that," JT joked.

In a more serious tone, Loretta says, "You need to talk to him soon. He is…"

JT quickly stops her in mid-sentence and pleads, "Mom, can you please stop with all that talk for a little while? Let's just enjoy this one, please."

"Alright, alright. But it's important. We have to make some huge decisions in the next couple of days."

"Important to you," he says under his breath. He's defiant, but respectful because he's aware of all that she has done for him.

In an effort to squelch the mounting tension, Tanya asks, "Are you going to ride home with us?"

JT replies, "No, I'm gonna ride in the van with the team. I'll see you back at the school though for the Pep Rally. You'll be there, right Ma?"

"We'll see. I've got to get your Auntie home."

A quick group hug ensues followed by another hip-high hug from Mikey. Loretta, then, grabs her first born and pulls him close and whispers up in the direction of his ear, "You know how proud I am of you, right?"

"I know, Ma. That's all I really want."

JT picks up his bag and slings it over his shoulder and begins walking toward the two passenger vans. Just as he reaches the van door, Loretta exclaims, "Love you, Son!"

A little embarrassed he turns to look back at her, and says, "I know, me too. I'll see you in a bit."

CHAPTER 9

The Championship celebration was pre-planned. As customary, following a Varsity Basketball road tournament win, the party would start in the locker room, continue during the van-ride home and be followed by an open pep-rally back at the school. The school's current administration feels it's important to share its successes with the students; since, for many of the kids, this is all they have.

The players, coaches and equipment are all stuffed into two oversized passenger vans. JT and his buddy, Stevie, are seated on a bench together in the second van, directly behind the driver's seat. JT insists on that window seat; all great athletes have their quirks and JT was starting to formulate his. The celebratory music blares from two portable speakers near the rear of the van.

Both vans embark from the Trinity Titan parking lot and begin their 30-minute journey back to Central City High School. Stevie rises up on one knee and turns to address his teammates in the back of the van. He yells, "Great win, Boys! Now, let's hear some Biggie Smalls!"

"You got it, Boss," was the loud reply, followed by seconds of silence as the music man sets up his playlist. As requested, explicit rap music begins to blast from the back of the van and the players continue to party. Stevie slides back down into his seat and begins rocking back and forth to the beat of the music.

Stevie pops JT on the shoulder and says loudly, over the sound of the music, "Can you believe that shit, Dog? We pulled that one out of our asses!"

"No doubt. Your last pass was dead on. Perfect, I'm telling ya," JT yells back. He leans in close for Stevie to hear, "I'm gonna miss playing with you the most."

"Yeah, me too. But, when ESPN comes to interview me before some NBA All-Star game about what it was like to play with you, I'll be able to say that I played with a BALLER!"

JT, humble as usual and almost embarrassed, throws an elbow into Stevie's side, "Man, speaking of that, my mom won't let up on me. She keeps pushing this Euro-pro thing."

"It's hard to blame her. That first year will be more paper than she'll make in her whole life."

"I know, but it's not all about the money for me. I don't think she really cares about what I want. You know, I probably never told you, but my Dad really wanted me to go to college and play ball. I kind of feel like I owe it to him. So, I'm just gonna tell her that tomorrow I'm officially committing to UK and be done with it." JT pauses as a feeling of pride fills his chest when he realizes that may be the first time he's actually said it out loud to someone other than his Mom. Confidently, he jokes, "What can she do, ground me?"

The party continues inside the vans as they approach the intersection to access the on-ramp for the highway that will take them North, to Downtown St. Louis. The first van makes the left turn on a green light and the second van follows closely behind. An approaching car, with loud thumping bass booming into the early evening air, races toward the intersection. Behind the wheel of this approaching car is a teenaged male driver who's fumbling with his cell phone, oblivious to the fact that the cars in front of his have obeyed the red traffic signal. He looks up from his phone just in time to steer his car to the right shoulder, avoiding a rear-end collision.

The momentum carries his car through the shoulder and into the intersection, toward the second van. Startled, the driver attempts to step on the brake but instead his foot slides to the gas pedal and he rapidly accelerates forward, slamming into the side of the second van. The van is pushed to the left side of the on-ramp, toward the embankment that is twenty-five feet above the busy highway below. The young driver successfully finds the brake pedal and hammers it to the floor. This stops the car's momentum and sends him into his steering wheel, as no airbag is deployed. That inertia transfers to the van and it spills over the guardrail. It begins to tumble down the embankment toward the rushing northbound traffic on the highway.

The collision came without warning to anyone. Screams of fear and pain ring out in the second van as it tumbles down the embankment. The seven passengers, including JT and Stevie, are spinning and colliding inside the van. JT's head smashes against the window of the van, it shatters but doesn't break. The skin on his head, just above his left ear, opens up from the impact. His right ankle is pinned under the seat as the van makes another revolution. JT shrieks out as the bones above his ankle snap like a dry twig.

As the van reaches the bottom of the embankment, it completes a second revolution and crashes to a halt. As it does, JT's head smashes against the same shattered window again. Moans and groans are heard, the screaming has stopped. Stevie, groggy from the impact, pulls himself up to survey the situation. He mutters aloud, "What the hell? Is everyone okay?"

The team trainer yells out, "Is anyone hurt? Someone call nine-one-one!"

Stevie realizes that he's alone, in a different seat, lying sideways. He calls out, "JT! Where's JT? We were sitting right next to each other."

JT replies, moaning through his words, "I'm right here. You must have gotten thrown. My foot is stuck and it hurts really bad. I think it's fuckin' broke!"

When the impact of the second van is heard, the first van screeches to a halt on the on-ramp to the highway. Its passengers, including Coach Miller, feverishly exit into the cold night air and make their way down the embankment. The once speeding traffic on the highway has come to a grinding halt. The second van lies on its side, in the ditch; it never reached the roadway.

After regaining his orientation inside the van, Stevie climbs over a seat and a pile of scattered gym bags to get to JT's side. As calmly as he can muster, he says to JT, "Don't move your head, Bro. You're cut pretty bad." Stevie looks around the wreckage for something to tamponade the bleeding from the gash on JT's head, like they learned in Health Class. Finding nothing within his arm's reach, he quickly removes his shirt and begins to apply direct pressure to the wound. He warns JT, "I'm gonna put some pressure here. Try to hold still."

JT, still in shock and confused, asks, "What happened?"

Taking in the chaos that's going on around them, Stevie replies, "I'm not really sure. We were talking one minute and then, BAM! Next thing I know, I'm over there. I think my wrist is broke, it hurts like a bitch." Stevie slowly lifts the shirt from JT's head wound to examine the cut, and says, "Damn, you're bleeding a lot."

JT says, "My head's throbbing. I feel like I'm gonna puke."

"Hold that shit in. How's your ankle?"

"Don't know, I can't really feel it; my head hurts too bad."

Coach Miller, not the healthiest of specimens, is out of breath from navigating his way down the embankment as he takes charge of the efforts outside the overturned van. He yells over to Dante, who is peering in the front windshield, "Dante, call nine-one-one!"

"I already did Coach, they're coming. I can see Stevie and JT, it looks pretty bad in there."

The Coach pulls on the back door from the outside, while one of the other boys pushes it open from the inside. The twisted metal door slowly creaks open after great force is applied and the less injured, but weary, make their way out of the wreckage. Coach Miller peers in the open door and says, "Hang in there, boys. Help is on the way."

The faint sound of sirens can be heard in the distance, getting closer with each passing second. Stevie leans in close to JT's ear, "How ya doing, Dog? Just hang on, they're on their way to help us."

His voice is getting weaker and frail. JT asks, "What

happened? Where are we?"

Stevie begins to wonder if it's more than just a cut on JT's head. He yells out to anyone that can hear him, "Tell them to hurry!"

JT says, in a faint whine, "Oh man, I don't..." He stops in mid-sentence. In an even weaker voice, he continues, "My head really hurts. Quit yelling."

The police arrive at the accident scene and the officers begin to set up a safety perimeter around the overturned van. Three of the deputies lay down flares on the highway pavement and begin to direct the slow-moving cars around the crash site. A firetruck and an ambulance are the next pieces of EMS equipment to arrive. The personnel work swiftly to gather the requisite equipment to manage the scene and the firefighters quickly stabilize the van to prevent shifting.

Most of the passengers from the second van have carefully made their way from the wreckage and first aid is being delivered to those in need. Stevie and JT are the only remaining victims in the van, but Stevie has shifted his attention to the EMS personnel. He's answering their questions through the open back door.

Stevie turns his concern back to JT. "Okay Dog, the medics are here and they're gonna get you out."

There is no response from JT, he's fallen unconscious.

"JT, can you hear me," he says in a louder voice while gently tapping JT's shoulder.

Nothing.

Stevie yells out again, this time in a panic-stricken voice, "Hey, he's not talking! JT stopped talking!"

Just then, a paramedic climbs through the back door of the van carrying a medic box. He gets up as close to JT's head as he can, given the cramped quarters. He takes JT's head into his hands to maintain his neck alignment while quickly palpating his neck, the right carotid artery, for a pulse.

"What's your buddy's name," the medic calmly asks Stevie.

"James, he goes by JT."

"Was he alert and talking?"

"A minute ago, he was. He just stopped answering me," Stevie explained.

While maintaining neck alignment with his hands the paramedic yells in JT's ear, "Hey JT, can you hear me?"

No response at all.

Knowing the dire progression of a head injured patient losing consciousness, the paramedic quickly explains to Stevie, "Okay, we've got to get him out of here and that starts by getting you out. Can you walk?"

"Yes, it's just my wrist that hurts."

"Why don't you slide on out so my partner can squeeze in here? We'll take good care of him, I promise."

"Okay, but check out his right ankle, it's stuck under this bench."

The paramedic says, "You did a great job managing this cut, thanks. We'll handle his ankle."

"Take care of him, Man," Stevie pleads as he makes his way out the back of the van.

The second paramedic enters the wreckage with a backboard, a neck brace and head supports. The first paramedic asks, "How much longer on that Medivac?"

"Should be here any minute."

The darkness of the night sky is interrupted by the contrasting brightness of the landing lights on the Medivac chopper as it approaches the scene. The police officers have stopped all traffic and created a makeshift landing area. The bird hovers just above the pavement and touches down gently like a seagull on the sand as the witnesses and bystanders shield themselves from the dust and debris stirred up by the whirling blades.

The two paramedics emerge from the wreckage with JT secured to their backboard. They quickly and carefully place him on the gurney and wheel him toward the running helicopter. The back-loading doors of the chopper are opened by the co-pilot. Together, he and the EMS team load JT into the back of the chopper. After just a few minutes of rapid preparation, the crew is ready for departure. As the helicopter lifts off and turns to the North, the Paramedic team returns to the overturned van with the empty gurney. Coach Miller and his boys stand by in shock, struggling to comprehend what they just witnessed.

Coach Miller pulls one of the Medics close and yells over the sound of the departing chopper, "Where are they taking him? I need to call his Mom."

"University Hospital, Downtown."

The Coach grabs the Paramedic by the arm and looks into his eyes with hope, and asks, "How is he?" The paramedic closes his eyes and shakes his head back and forth, answering the question without a verbal response.

The helicopter engines are loud and the quarters are tight inside the flying intensive care unit. JT's body and head are secured tightly to the sled as the flight nurse and flight medic work diligently trying to assess JT's injuries and perform life saving measures. The laceration on his head has received a field dressing and the bleeding is controlled.

Each of them is wearing headphones with microphones for better communication. After securing JT's airway with an endotracheal tube, the flight nurse osculates his chest with her stethoscope. She speaks into her microphone, as she attaches the ventilator tubing, "Okay, the breathing tube is in." She continues to examine JT's eyes with an extremely bright pen light. She pries his eyes open, one at a time, shining the light on them and looking for a pupillary response. She reports her findings, "His right pupil is a three and brisk. His left pupil is fixed and dilated, no reaction to light."

The Flight Medic responds to the nurse's report, "This is not looking good." He turns to address the pilot and speaks into his headset microphone, "Can you make this thing fly any faster?"

The Medivac chopper cuts through the dark, chilly night sky with JT's life in the balance.

CHAPTER 10

Mikey Stone has acquired the ability to keep himself entertained these last few years. It's not that Loretta doesn't make time for him, it's related more to the limited time that she has to provide. Because of the busy schedules of the two older members of the household, Mikey has created a world of his own. His imagination is vibrant and quite creative and he uses it to pass the time when he finds himself alone at home. He can take the simplest household item and manufacture, in his mind, a world around it complete with inhabitants and storylines. Loretta often jokes with him about being the smartest boy in the house.

Mikey's recollection of his Daddy is limited, mostly made up of vague memories and stories his Mother would share. Mikey had just celebrated his sixth birthday, when James passed away. His death brought with it some serious behavior issues for Mikey, especially at school. The main problem was with male authority figures, two specific teachers to be exact. The school counselor contended that there was an "abandonment issue" and suggested therapy. Loretta chose to dismiss that suggestion in favor of feeding the boys on a regular basis. The therapy that she had in mind didn't involve paying to lay on a couch and hypnosis, but rather homeschooling by a tutor and courtside seats.

———————————

An unusual silence fills the car and both women are content taking full advantage of it; a stark contrast to the raucous environment they were in just sixty minutes ago. Mikey is sprawled across the backseat playing with two Transformer action figures, re-enacting a scene from the movie he saw during last summer break. Tanya is sitting quietly in the passenger seat as Loretta pulls into the entrance to Tanya's West County neighborhood.

The silence is broken with the ringing of Loretta's cell phone. Tanya pulls Loretta's purse onto her lap and begins digging through it. "How can you find anything in here? I hear it, but I sure can't see it," she says.

"Well, answer it," Loretta orders.

Tanya delivers a scowl in Loretta's direction, as if offended by her instruction. She locates the device, flips it open and aggressively says, "Hello?"

The male voice on the other end of the line is that of Coach Miller. Trying to convey a calm demeanor, he says, "Loretta, is this you?"

Tanya replies, "No, this is her sister. Who's this?"

"It's Duane Miller."

"Who," she asks.

"Coach Miller. Can I please speak to Ms. Stone? It's important."

"Hold on, she's driving."

Hearing only one side of that conversation, Loretta asks, "Who is it?"

Covering the phone's mouthpiece, she says, "It's Coach Miller, he says it's important."

"Well, see what he wants." Concern takes over as she begins to wonder why he would be calling. Loretta says, "Actually, hold on. I'll pull over."

Tanya speaks into the cell phone, "Hang on Coach, Loretta is pulling the car over." Loretta quickly pulls the car off onto the side of the street, about three-hundred yards from Tanya's house.

"Here, let me see that phone," Loretta says as she reaches across the seats. "Hello, this is Loretta."

"Loretta, there's been an accident," the Coach reports.

"Accident? What accident?"

"JT's van. I don't know how bad it is but they took him to University Hospital in a helicopter."

Loretta, in shock, replies, "My JT? In a helicopter?"

"You need to get there as soon as you can," the coach adds.

Shock turns to panic. "We're on our way." Loretta slaps

the flip phone shut and tries to tell Tanya the news but is unable to formulate her words.

Tanya interjects, "What was that about?"

"JT was…," she continues to stumble. "He's at University Hospital. We need to get there now."

Tanya, noticing the condition that her sister is in, unbuckles her seatbelt and says, "I'll drive, you're in no shape."

Moving in slow motion, Loretta releases her seatbelt but is unable to summon the strength to move as those words ring in her head like a cannon shot. Tanya opens the driver's door and helps Loretta exit the car. She places her in the passenger seat and climbs behind the wheel. As they are in the process of switching seats, Mikey is pulled out of his imaginary play land and becomes alarmed. He questions them, "Hey, what's going on? Why are you guys switching? Mama, why are you crying?"

Tanya replies on Loretta's behalf as she pulls her car back on the street. "Your brother was hurt in an accident."

Trying to compose herself and summon the strength within her to be strong for Mikey, Loretta says, "We really don't know much, so let's not get too worked up. We'll see him when we get there." Meanwhile, the worst of the worst thoughts pour into her head. She begins to silently cry.

Together, the sisters begin to pray out loud as Tanya directs the car out of her neighborhood and speeds off toward the unknown.

CHAPTER 11

A red hue from the illuminated EMERGENCY sign fills the night sky and casts itself like a fog over the parking lot. An ambulance crew is unloading another unfortunate patient inside the ambulance bay as Loretta's car pulls into the area reserved for emergency room parking.

Loretta has spent the last twenty minutes torturing herself, playing out the potential details of the accident in her mind. She wonders what his injuries could be; why a helicopter? She tries to convince herself that it could be nothing more than a precautionary measure. How will I pay for this? What about our future? Each of these are valid concerns.

As Tanya pulls the car up near the Emergency Room entrance, Loretta flings the passenger door open even before the car screeches to a halt. Fearing the worst, but praying for the best, Loretta's feet barely touch the ground as she sprints inside the door.

The registration area is full of patients and loved ones, waiting to be seen. Loretta approaches the desk with panic and desperation in her eyes. A young female ER nurse is sitting behind the reception desk; the gatekeeper between those who need and those who provide healthcare.

As Loretta hurriedly arrives at the desk, she begins, "Where's my baby? He was in a car accident!"

The nurse extends her arms as if directing traffic, and says, "Calm down ma'am and I'll try to help you. What's the patient's name?"

"His name is JT Stone, James Stone! He was brought here by helicopter!"

The young lady reviews the information on her computer terminal, and asks, "What's your relation to the patient?"

"I'm his Mama!"

Reading the honesty in her terrified face, she says to Loretta, "Yes ma'am, he's here. Please stay right here and I'll go check on his status." The ER employee disappears through two swinging doors.

Tanya and Mikey rush into the reception area and to Loretta's side. "What's going on," Tanya asks.

"That girl went to go see. Why doesn't she know?"

Tanya replies, "Hang tight, Lo. She'll be right back and then we'll get to see him."

After just a few minutes, the ER nurse pushes through the doors with a new-found urgency. She says, "I'm going to take you to a consultation room and one of our ER doctors will update you."

Loretta begins pushing for answers, "Where's my boy? Why won't you just tell me?"

Pleading her case, she says, "Please, just follow me. I don't really know the details."

They enter a small consultation room, made even smaller by the enormity of the situation. The young nurse says, "Please, have a seat in here. The doctor will be right in." As she quickly turns to exit the room, she runs directly into one of the ER doctors. "Actually, here he is now. This is Dr. Sanderson."

He's hardly the seasoned professional they expected to see; he looks like he just stepped out of the classroom. The young doctor enters the room and motions for each of them to take a seat. As they do, he begins, "Good evening, Ma'am. Are you the mother of the victim?" Just as the word "victim" leaves his mouth, he realizes his faux pas.

Loretta, sternly, jumps all over that. "Victim? What are you talking about? I'm Ms. Stone, JT's Mother!" The distrust is building quickly. Tears begin to fill her eyes.

His apology was immediate. "I'm so sorry. I only meant the victim in the accident. Of course, I'm sorry." He stammers on, "I'm Dr. Sanderson, I am one of the doctors that attended to your son when he arrived."

Already disgusted with this conversation, Loretta insists, "Why don't you just tell me what's going on and where he is?"

"James was…," he began, but was interrupted by Loretta.

"He goes by JT."

Dr. Sanderson nods his head in acknowledgement and continues, "JT was involved in a car accident and has suffered multiple injuries. The worst of which is an injury to his head."

Tanya and Loretta grab each other and strain to hear every word the physician is saying. Mikey is in shock, not saying a word.

The doctor continues, "JT has an ankle fracture which will be dealt with later. It's the head injury that we're focused on now."

Tanya asks, "Can we see him?"

"Well, no. He's currently in the operating room where a brain surgeon is…,"

Loretta, with escalating concern, interrupts the young doctor again, "Wait! Operating room? Brain Surgeon?"

"Yes, ma'am. Dr. Childers is working on him as we speak. During the accident, JT must have hit his head against something that has caused bleeding inside his brain. The surgeon had to go in to stop the bleeding and relieve the pressure."

Loretta sits, frozen in disbelief. Her mouth is agape

while trying to process these words. Mikey emerges from his state of shock and manages to verbalize his primary question, one that they all secretly wanted to ask, "Is my brother going to die? He can't die!" He quickly becomes tearful at the thought of life without his hero. Tanya consoles him with a loving embrace.

Loretta slides to her knees, in front of Mikey, and grabs his hands. "No baby, our JT isn't going to die. God won't let that happen to us."

Dr. Sanderson continues, "Ms. Stone, you're welcome to stay in here as long as you'd like. Or, I can have someone take you up to the surgical waiting area. That's where the neurosurgeon will be looking for family when he's finished."

Wiping tears from her cheeks while she rises to her feet to face the doctor, Loretta answers, "Okay, we'll go there. What did you say about his ankle?"

"It's his right ankle. It's fractured and has been set temporarily, but will need to be surgically repaired down the road."

"I hope it's not a bad break. You know, he's going to the NBA." Denial has already begun for Loretta.

"I'm sure they'll do all they can. Wait right here and that young lady will take you upstairs." Dr. Sanderson leaves the room without a word of thanks from anyone.

When Loretta, Tanya and Mikey are brought into a large open surgical waiting area by the same ER nurse they finally see a familiar face, Coach Duane Miller. A slight sense of relief is felt for the first time since the phone call. The Coach stands to greet them, surrounded by several members of the basketball team that have come to show their support.

As she approached them, the coach says, "Loretta, I'm so sorry this happened."

"How did it happen? I still haven't gotten the whole story."

Trying hard to spare her the details, he motions for Stevie to come join them. He deflects her question by saying, "Stevie was in the van with JT."

As Stevie approaches, Loretta notices that his right arm is tightly wrapped and secured by a sling around his neck. She gives him a gentle, motherly hug. "Oh, sweetie, your arm. Are you okay?"

"Yes, ma'am, I'll be fine. Doc says it's just a sprain. Honestly, I don't even care about it at this point." Stevie begins choking on his emotions as he recalls the horrific crash. "It all happened so fast. All I know is that JT took the brunt of it. It's just not fair. One minute he was talking to me and the next minute he wasn't. I'm really scared." Stevie begins to weep openly for the first time since the accident.

Loretta reaches forward and carefully pulls Stevie in

close and consoles him in her motherly way. "It's okay, Stevie. All that matters now is that they put my boy back together." Loretta releases her hold on Stevie and speaks directly to Coach Miller, "Coach, it's so late. You and the boys should be getting back home. You don't need to be here. I'll keep you posted."

"Well, I agree that the boys should, but I'd like to stay here with you. I can't leave him, he's like a son to me."

"I know he'd appreciate you being here. But, at this hour, I really think you need to get these boys back to their families."

The Coach nods his head in agreement, recognizing his obligations to the entire team.

Stevie asks, "Ms. Stone, can I please stay? JT's my boy."

"Does your Mama know what happened and that you're okay?"

"Yes Ma'am. I just talked to her. She said I could stay as long as I stay out of your hair. I promise I will."

Loretta says, "Son, don't you worry about that now. I know that you and JT are buddies, but I really think it's best that you get back home." She reaches for his good hand, "I know your Mama, and I know she wants to wrap her arms around you tonight. So, please go on home."

Coach Miller puts his arm around Stevie's shoulder and

gives him a loose squeeze. "I agree with her, son. Let's get you and the boys home. We'll all come see him in a couple days."

Loretta silently mouths a "Thank you" to Coach Miller and then addresses the group of young men by saying, "Thank you all for being here for JT. I'll let him know you were here."

Coach Miller rounds up the guys and walks them toward the exit. Their collective pace is slow and lethargic, more like a funeral march. Their demeanors have changed, contrary to the celebration they had a few short hours ago.

CHAPTER 12

Whoever said "waiting is the hardest part" nailed that on the head, Loretta thought to herself as she sat in the softly lit room designated for just that purpose. A hospital can be a quiet place in the middle of the night except for the occasional overhead page for some doctor to go somewhere, STAT. The last time Loretta was in a situation like this she was waiting on news about her husband's fate. It's a hopeless feeling to not know what lies ahead for you, to have your future in the hands of total strangers. Loretta can't help but recall that day when she found herself a widowed mother of two young boys.

She vowed, secretly, that day that she would take charge of their lives and make decisions that would give them the best chance at survival. Deep down inside her, she knows that's why she's pushing so hard for JT to go to the NBA as soon as he possibly can. This would guarantee a future for them all. But, now this. "How will this affect that," she silently ponders as she looks across the room at her baby boy in the arms of her only other true support, Tanya.

Loretta's ringing cell phone jars her from a state of inner reflection. She reaches down and grabs her purse that's on the floor next to the couch. Pulling the phone from the purse, she reads the screen aloud, "Trina Kelley. What could she want at this hour?" Loretta flips the phone open and walks toward the picture window that overlooks the city lights of St. Louis. "Trina, is that you?"

Trina's disheveled red hair hangs from her head like a loose mop. Apparently, there is no time to clean oneself up after being awoken by the sound of a suffocating human being, especially when it's your spouse who's lying in the bed next to you.

The doctor's predictions were correct, her husband's health was declining rapidly. Trina summoned the ambulance as soon as she heard Bryan's gasping breaths. A breathing treatment and high flow oxygen got him to the emergency department where he is now receiving advanced airway therapy just to keep him stable. They were out of the woods, for now. These emergency visits have been more frequent and more intense these past few months.

Trina replies, "Yeah, it's me. I'm so sorry to wake you at this hour. Can you talk?" She is running her fingers through the hair of her frail-appearing husband as he lays on the exam bed, inside the tight quarters of the ER room. The panic on his face, as he struggles for oxygen, equals the panicked tone of Trina's voice.

Loretta replies, "Well, actually, I wasn't...,"

Trina interrupts, in a hurry to get her own news across.

114

"We're in the ER at University. I had to call an ambulance."

"Slow down, Trina. How bad…," the verbal intrusions continue.

"Worst one yet." She tearfully continues, "I'm really scared."

Loretta says, "Oh dear, I'm so sorry." She paused for a moment to reflect on what Trina said. "Wait, did you say University Hospital?"

"Yeah."

"We're here too."

"Why, what's wrong," Trina asked.

"My JT was in a car accident."

Trina replied, "No. What happened?"

Loretta's tears slowly build in her eyes and spill over onto her cheeks at the very thought of it all. "It was a car accident. I haven't been able to see him yet. He's still in surgery."

"Oh, my God, Loretta. I'm so sorry to hear that."

"I'm just upstairs from you, in the Neurosurgical Waiting Room. We should…"

Trina's attention was diverted away from her conversation by the entrance of one the ER physicians into their room. Trina says, "Lo, I need to call you back later. Bryan's doctor just walked in."

"Okay, Honey. Let's say some prayers for each other."

"Yes, please. I'll find you tomorrow."

Loretta closes her phone and walks back toward the couch, her couch for the night. It's not exactly comfortable, but it's serving a purpose. She surveys the room and appreciates that her conversation had not stirred Tanya or Mikey. Rather than curl up alone, Loretta decided to join her family on the larger couch across the room. The thought of snuggling up with her family brought a comfort to her. It's just what the doctor would have ordered.

CHAPTER 13

There are many plausible reasons; the late hour, the darkened room or even the silence around them, but sheer exhaustion was the likely cause for their slumber. It's not as if anyone could blame them. Loretta tried hard to fight off the Sandman that night but was unable. The trio was sharing an extra-long couch in the surgical waiting room when JT's doctor came looking for them.

Dr. Barkley Childers is a brain surgeon, just breaking into his fifties. He's a full partner and a founding member of his private practice, Midwest Neurosurgical Partners. Certainly, wealthy enough not to have to be on call anymore; he does it because he loves his career and his chosen field. Besides, he's a surgeon, he loves to cut. He has a reputation around the hospital, especially with the junior staff, for being a straight-shooter and having a bedside manner that some patients just don't appreciate. But in the end, that's not what saves lives.

Dr. Childers enters the surgical waiting area with one of the Neurosurgical ICU nurses, Jennifer, and approaches Loretta's couch. He reaches out and gently touches her shoulder, "Ms. Stone? Are you Ms. Stone?"

Loretta opens her eyes and sits upright in her seat, shaking the confusion from her head. She responds, "Yes, yes I am." She reaches over and pinches Tanya who is lying in the opposite direction, on the same couch. "Sissy, the doctor's here."

Mikey, undisturbed by the conversation, is still asleep next to Tanya. He can sleep through a tornado. Tanya says, "Let me get Mikey up."

"No, let him sleep, it's okay," Loretta whispers back.

"Ms. Stone," the doctor continues. "I'm Dr. Childers. I just finished operating on your son, James. Just so I know, how much have you been told about his injuries?"

"Not much, really. We know he hit his head and needed surgery and that his ankle is broken."

The physician understands that not much was divulged to them because not much was known at the time. However, the burden now falls on him to provide the unfortunate details.

"How is he? When can we see him," Loretta asked.

Dr. Childers believes in good news first. So, in a very dry, direct and matter-of-fact manner, he said, "Let me start by saying that your son is alive." The severity of this statement hits Loretta like a gut punch from Mike Tyson. "He has suffered a severe brain injury." Loretta is stunned by that statement as well - a crushing left hook from Iron

118

Mike. Without interruption, mostly because Loretta is speechless, he continues. "Upon arrival to the hospital, your son was unresponsive. The CT Scan showed a large area of bleeding inside his head, which required emergent surgery. In the operating room, we found two areas of bleeding and a large hematoma that formed and occluded blood flow to a portion of his brain. The long-term damage done to that area is uncertain at this time. He has been taken to the Neurosurgical Intensive Care Unit for close monitoring." Shocked silence fills the room. "Do you have any questions?"

Loretta begins stammering her words. She can barely formulate a question, but she manages to generate two of them, "What do you mean by uncertain? Why don't you know?"

The surgeon attempts to explain, "It's impossible for me to predict how he will respond to the surgical interventions. The next few hours are critical. There is another, a more serious complication from his injury that you need to be aware of."

"It gets worse," Loretta asks with a sarcastic slant.

"We do expect there to be further swelling inside his brain, which is being addressed with medications."

Loretta and Tanya share blank stares, in disbelief.

Nearly two minutes pass without a word from anyone.

Seeming like no time at all to the sisters, the awkwardness of the situation feels like an eternity to Dr. Childers. He breaks the silence, "Please forgive me for being brief. If you have no further questions, I have to go to the ER to see another patient. I'll be back up to check on his condition in a little while. Jennifer, one of our Neuro ICU nurses, will take you to see James now."

Dr. Childers turns and starts walking away. Loretta says, in a soft helpless voice, "His name is JT."

The doctor turns back to acknowledge her comment, "Excuse me?"

Her passive-aggressive nature takes over. In a louder, stern voice, she says, "His name is James Stone. He likes to be called JT."

He nods his head in her direction and says, "Thank you for correcting me." As he turns toward the exit he quietly says to himself, "God, I hate that part."

Tanya turns on the couch to face Loretta and they embrace, consoling each other as they attempt to absorb the doctor's words. Loretta says, "Maybe I'm just tired and cranky, but how is it that he can operate on someone's brain but he can't explain things very well?"

"Loretta, don't say that. Did you hear him; JT's alive. He saved his life!" She pauses for a moment and continues.

"I know you hate hospitals and most people in them but have some respect for that man."

Jennifer, their nurse for the remainder of the night, steps forward to offer some insight. "Before we go back to see JT, I want you both to know that while Dr. Childers may not have the greatest bedside manner, he is the best neurosurgeon in this hospital." She pauses to consider her comment. "Probably the whole state. He is definitely who you want driving this bus right now."

Loretta shows no remorse for her comment.

Jennifer continues, "Now, if you'll follow me, I'll take you to see JT now."

Tanya gently wakes Mikey up and scoops him into her arms. Loretta gathers their belongings and they follow Jennifer out of the waiting room and down the hall toward the Neuro ICU.

CHAPTER 14

The Neuro Intensive Care Unit of University Hospital is an award-winning facility. The Unit houses state-of–the-art technologies and the best-trained group of neurosurgical nurses in the city. It sees the worst of the head injuries because of the Level One designation the hospital has earned. In addition to the trauma patients, the unit cares for those patients who have suffered anything from acute strokes to the most complex of brain surgeries. People travel from all over the country to be treated by Dr. Childers and the Neurosurgical team that serves the St. Louis community. JT has made it this far; into the hands of a truly gifted surgeon and under the care of a top-ranked team.

The family group reluctantly enters the dimly-lit intensive care room to the rhythmic sound of the ventilator; the ebb and flow of air being pushed into and out of JT's lungs. He lies motionless in the hospital bed, except for the rise and fall of his chest. Tubes and wires are protruding from his body as a wall of IV pumps infuse medications into his bloodstream. No outward signs of trauma can be seen except for the surgical dressing surrounding his head and the oversized splint on his broken right ankle.

Loretta raises her hand over her mouth and mutters, "Oh, my baby." She begins to weep.

Tanya slides Mikey down her side, onto his feet. He quickly grabs his Momma's waist and Tanya wraps her arms around Loretta. The family embraces as if holding each other up at the sight of their "rock" lying helpless in that bed.

Tanya asks Jennifer, "Can you please explain what all this stuff is? In simple terms, please."

"I'll try. Currently, we have him in a drug-induced coma," she began.

Loretta speaks out, "Did you say, coma?"

"Yes, we're giving him medication so that he is in a very deep sleep. This is done in an effort to decrease any further swelling inside his head. That's also why it's so dark in here and why we ask you not to stimulate him."

Loretta says, "When will he wake up?"

"We, honestly, don't know yet. At this point, we have to wait and see."

Mikey, curiously, is standing on his tip-toes straining to look over the bed rail at his brother. He pulls himself up on the bed rail and asks, "Why are his eyes so puffy?"

Tanya interjects, "Mikey, don't say that."

"No, that's a fair question," Jennifer says. As she kneels down to get closer to Mikey's eye level, she explains, "Mikey, have you ever twisted your ankle before?"

He shyly responds, "No, but my brother has."

"Do you remember that it got puffy and maybe turned black and blue after a while?"

"Yeah."

"Well, that's kind of the same thing that's going on here. Except, it's his head that is hurt instead of his ankle. Does that make sense?"

Mikey, quietly, looks back at Jennifer, "Yeah, I guess so." He grabs his Mother's waist again even tighter and begins to cry. He then says, "But, his ankle got better." The young boy turns his head and burrows into Loretta's side to hide his tears. She gently caresses his head.

Jennifer stands back up to further address the adults. "We will be continuously monitoring him for any changes."

"Thank you for explaining all of this to us," Tanya says. "Loretta, do you have any questions for the nurse?"

"No, I guess I don't. Not right now anyway."

Jennifer walks around the bed toward the series of IV pumps and begins adjusting the flow rate of one of the medications. She says to the group, "You're welcome to go back out to the waiting room. We will come out to get you if anything changes."

Almost insulted by this comment, Loretta rebuts, "Excuse me? I'm not going to the waiting room. This is my son lying here fighting for his life. He needs his Momma right here!"

"I didn't mean anything bad by that, Ms. Stone. It's just that we can't have everyone in here all at once. It can get pretty crowded in here and we may need to move quickly to address sudden changes in JT's condition. It's more about safety than anything."

"I can appreciate that, but I'd rather be in here."

Jennifer laments, "Okay, you can stay. But, we need to keep it to two visitors at a time." She walks out of the room and begins talking with two other nurses just outside the room. They are looking back into the room at JT's vital signs monitor, clearly discussing his condition.

Tanya speaks up, "You know what, Loretta? I think I'll take Mikey back to my house, he's exhausted. We'll come back up after some sleep and a good breakfast."

"Okay, that's a great idea. He's been so good through all of this." Straining to recall, Loretta says, "Wait, today's Monday. I'll call Mikey's school in a few hours. There's no way I'm sending him to school like this." Loretta and Tanya embrace in a hug that has more meaning than any other between them.

"Love you, sis," Tanya says. Tears stream down Loretta's face as they hug.

"I love you too. Thank you, for everything."

Loretta squats down in front of Mikey and wraps her

motherly arms around him, squeezing him tightly. "You go with your Auntie and get some good sleep. I'm gonna stay here so when JT wakes up he'll know we're here."

"Okay, Mommy. Tell him that I said to get better."

"I will baby, I will."

Tanya walks over to JT's bedside and softly touches his hand. She drops to her knees and silently says a prayer. When finished, she stands, takes Mikey's hand and leads him out of the room before she breaks down.

Loretta slowly makes her way to the foot of JT's hospital bed, as she quietly surveys the room. These are images that she never imagined or even wanted to see. She can't help but recall how eerily similar they are to the ones already there from her husband's hospitalization. They bring back emotions from what was, prior to this day, the worst day of her life. She is standing guard over her son's hospital bed as if she will be able to protect him from what she can't even see – the pressure building inside his head. Looking deeply into his face, she mutters, "Looks like it's just you and me kid. I'll protect you."

Jennifer re-enters the room with another nurse, Melissa. Together, they will be responsible for JT's care for the night. A normal assignment for an ICU nurse on any given shift is two patients. Because of the serious nature of JT's injuries and the instability in his condition, the inverse ratio of normal will be required tonight. Jennifer offers the introduction, "Ms. Stone, this is Melissa. She's also a nurse here in the ICU. She and I will be taking care of your son for the rest of the night."

"Hi Ms. Stone," Melissa says. "Here, let's pull this chair up closer to the bed so you can sit with your son. It's okay to touch his hand, but please try not to stimulate him too much."

"Thank you, both." In her own way, she offers them special thanks by saying, "You girls can call me Loretta."

As the nurses tend to JT, Loretta inches the chair as close as possible to the bed. She cradles her son's hand into hers and examines its details as if trying to memorize every line and crease. She begins to tearfully whisper, "Please come back to me, JT. I'm so sorry for pushing you. I promise that I'll back off. Just please come back to us."

Loretta tenderly rests her forehead against the soft, snowy-white blanket that covers the bed. Slowly and tranquilly, she succumbs to her exhaustion.

CHAPTER 15

The early morning sun creeps its way through the window of JT's ICU room, warmly caressing Loretta's face. She hasn't moved since falling asleep several hours ago. Startled by the amount of activity in the room, she opens her eyes and sits straight up in her bedside chair. The cramping pain from her knotted up back awakens her completely to her nightmare, reality.

Jennifer and Melissa are trying to be stealthily quiet as they expertly go about their clinical duties. Dr. Childers stands at JT's head examining his eyes with a tiny, but extremely bright penlight. Giving his verbal instructions to the nurses, the doctor says, "Melissa, let's turn that Levophed drip off and start a Vasopressin drip. I'll put the order in shortly."

Realizing that their activities have caused Loretta to wake, he acknowledges her by saying, "Ah, good morning Ms. Stone. Sorry to startle you. JT's nurses have called me to his bedside with some concerns."

As Loretta stands and stretches, in an effort to loosen her back, she rubs her eyes clear of the fog and pleads in a panicked voice, "What is it? What's wrong?"

The surgeon begins to explain his valid concerns, "The hourly neuro exams that the nurses have been performing are showing some significant changes. These are rather troubling." He gestures to the bedside monitor that displays JT's vital signs, beat-by-beat, and continues, "In addition, his blood pressure and the degree of pressure inside his head are on the rise."

JT continues to lay motionless on the bed. On the outside, things appear unchanged, while a war is raging inside his skull. Loretta stands and walks around the bed closer to the doctor and the monitor, trying to get a better focus on the entire situation. She places her hand on JT's arm and with extreme anxiety in her voice, she asks, "What does that mean?"

Dr. Childers calmly replies, "It means that his brain is continuing to swell, it means that his condition is getting worse." He places his hand on Loretta's arm and says, "In addition, he has stopped responding to us in any way."

"I thought you said he was in a drug coma."

"Yes ma'am, he was. I had the nurses turn off those sedating medications several hours ago while you were sleeping. The doses were low to begin with and the effects of those drugs have cleared his system by now. Yet, he's still not responding."

She sternly asks, "What are you going to do to fix it?"

"We've done and continue to do all that we can, both surgically and medically. Despite all of these aggressive efforts, his swelling is such that it is causing irreversible damage to his brain."

"So, you're telling me that there's nothing that can be done?" Loretta drops her head in defeat and begins shaking it back and forth. "I can't believe I'm hearing this, again!" She fights back a flood of tears and emotions, paramount of these is anger. She explains, "Dr. Childers, three years ago, a heart doctor told me there was nothing more that could be done to help my husband and he died. That day!" Her tears break through and her tone softens, "Are you telling me that my boy is going to die?"

"Ms. Stone, I'm telling you that we are doing everything within our power to save him."

Loretta drops to her knees at her son's bedside and begins sobbing uncontrollably. Melissa rushes to Loretta's side, trying to support and console her. Unfortunately, no amount of support will ever be enough. Her dreams of escaping her life are slipping away, along with her son. Loretta begins to pray aloud, "No, please Lord, don't let this be happening to my baby. We have so much left to do. I'll do anything you ask of me, just please don't take my son from me."

Dr. Childers, unnoticed, gets Jennifer's attention and

motions for her to follow him out of the room. He leads her away from the open door to JT's room, where he knows Loretta cannot hear his words. "I'm afraid that he has herniated his brain stem. I'll be back in a bit to do a formal exam."

"I was afraid of that, too," she says as she nods her head in agreement. "His neuro changes, overall assessment and vital signs have been on a roller coaster ride for hours."

"Yes, and now all that has stopped, a bad sign indeed," the doctor continued. He begins to walk toward the doors of the ICU, then he turns and says, "Before you guys change shifts, please make the call to MDN."

Jennifer responds, "I'll have everything ready and we'll make the referral."

CHAPTER 16

Kevin Mills is quite the dedicated company man. Most days that he's on-call he goes into the office to get paperwork done or even to just make an appearance. This day is no different except, this day, he will get to see his wife in the afternoon. There's a little extra pep in his step that's for sure, and everyone seems to notice.

Halfway through the morning the inevitable happens. While sitting at his desk in his little cubicle, pecking away at his keyboard seek and find style – showing his age - his pager starts chirping. It was really just a matter of time, and he knew it. Kevin reaches for the noise-maker on his hip and declares, "Damn, I was really hoping it would be quiet today." He takes the digital display pager from his hip and reads the screen. He bargains with himself by saying, "Okay, well maybe it will be a quick call, some donor lab results or something simple."

Rather than calling the number on the pager, Kevin decides to stretch his legs and walk to the Communications Center at the front of the building, where the page originated. With coffee mug in hand, he's greeted with friendly salutations from other office staff that he passes along the way.

Upon his arrival to the Communication Center, that darkened phone and computer headquarters, Kevin finds three staff members managing the referrals for the morning. He knocks on the open door to gain their attention. One of the high back swivel chairs turns slowly toward the door to reveal his favorite - Amy Mann. She says in a surprised voice, "Oh, hey there Kevin. I just paged you."

"Yeah, I was at my desk. What do you have for me?"

"There's a potential donor referral at University Hospital."

He jokingly says, "Well, at least it's close." Kevin is never one to complain about his work, he can put a positive spin on just about anything. He continues, "Do you know if they've done exams yet?"

"I'm not sure."

"Consent for donation?"

"Sorry, Kev, they didn't give me all those details." Amy hands over the referral sheet. "But, I did call the Family Support Liaison. I spoke with Melanie and she said that she was already at the hospital doing a follow up from a case last week. She also said that she'll look over the chart and give you a call shortly."

"Thanks for the info, Amy. I'll just head that way."

A classic Beatles tune can be heard blaring from the car's speakers as Kevin pulls into the parking lot of the large metropolitan hospital. He's always been a fan of the "Boys from Liverpool" and has developed this peculiar practice of listening to their music when preparing for a case. Similar in practice to JT, every star player has their eccentricities. The music is interrupted by the ringing of his cell phone through the car speakers. The display on the stereo reads, "MELANIE PRECISSI-CELL". He answers the call by pressing a button on the steering wheel. "Hey Melanie, I've been expecting your call. What's going on?"

Melanie's voice can be heard through the speakers inside the BMW, "Hey there, Kevin. Well, this is gonna be a tough one. He's an eighteen-year-old, African-American male that was involved in a rollover MVA. What I can tell from the chart is that he has a severe head injury and a fractured ankle."

"No other injuries," Kevin curiously asks.

"Nope," she replies.

"Have they done a brain death exam?"

"Yes, it was completed by Dr. Childers, but he has not yet discussed the findings with the family. You should probably come on down here."

Kevin replies, "Actually, I'm just pulling into the parking lot now. Have you had any family contact?"

"Nope, it's too early. There are a few family members here now. His mom is really having a hard time."

In a calm assuring voice, Kevin says, "Well, I'm glad that you're on the case then. She's going to need your expertise."

"Awe, thanks Kevin. Yours too. See you soon."

Kevin disconnects the call as he pulls into a parking spot. After sliding the shifter forward into the "P" position, he picks up his phone and taps on the screen to dial the cell phone number for his wife. Over the speakers, the ring tones reverberate through the car. After three rings, a voice mail message begins. "Hi, you've reached the voice mailbox of Sherry Mills. I am unable to answer…"

His bride's voice brings a huge smile to his face.

―――――――――――――

Sherry sits in her car outside a doctor's office building, her last appointment for the day. The engine is running and the radio is off. Her leg is bouncing to the sound of silence as she impatiently stares at the cell phone in her hand, waiting for the alert indicating the arrival of Kevin's intentional voice mail message. The tone sounds and she eagerly presses the requisite buttons on her screen to retrieve the message. A bright smile crosses her face when she hears the familiar voice of her husband, "Hi Sherry, it's me. Really sorry, but I may not make it this afternoon. I'm checking on a referral at University. So, it may be later tonight if the case doesn't go, or it could be tomorrow if it does. You know the drill." There's a relatively long pause in the message, then his voice continues, "Please keep an open mind. We may have some *other options*."

Her avoidance of the call was deliberate. She knew the drill alright; she figured it was going to be just another work-related excuse for missing their appointment. However, her hesitation served her very well this time because she was not expecting to hear him reference her word, "options".

Hearing him verbally stress the word has taken her off guard and she begins to wonder if he knew that she has been up to something. Ashamed, Sherry places the phone in her lap and covers her face with her hands.

CHAPTER 17

Dr. Childers is nearing the end of his 24-hour call rotation and he has that look about him; tired and a bit disheveled, but not out of it by any means. He returns to the Neuro ICU after seeing another ill-fated patient in the Emergency Department. This one, however, will likely recover from her stroke due to his rapid intervention.

Sleep is not something that he's had since the previous day. JT's surgery is what started his "24 hours of service," as he likes to call it.

After his third, and necessary, change of scrubs, he's wearing a tight-fitting surgical cap and some light-blue scrubs under his white lab coat. As the fatigued surgeon approaches the nurse's station, he scribbles feverishly onto a three-by-five index card (his sophisticated filing system) without wasting time to raise his head. He asks loudly, for anyone to answer, "Where's Jennifer?"

Courtney, a veteran and extremely trusted member of the Neuro ICU nursing staff, emerges from JT's room scouring her hands with sanitizing foam. Loretta, Tanya and Mikey can be seen through the glass door seated at JT's side. Courtney replies, "Her shift ended a while ago and she went home. I took over for her, Dr. Childers."

Looking up from his note card system, he acknowledges her, "Oh, hi Courtney. I'm glad you're here. The next few hours around here are going to be difficult."

"That's what I've heard. What can I do?"

He asks, "Has the apnea test I ordered for Mr. Stone been completed?"

"Yes, the results of the arterial blood gases, before and after the test, are there on the chart."

In a patient with normal lung function and no brain injury, Carbon Dioxide (CO_2) is maintained at normal levels by the body's ability to breath and effectively exhale that toxic gas. The brain is what regulates the body's drive to breath; when CO_2 levels reach dangerous concentrations in the blood stream, the brain is what tells the lungs to breath faster to exhale the gas. An arterial blood sample is the best way to measure CO_2 levels, after the lungs have had a chance to exhale that gas through the act of breathing.

At University Hospital, the established and accepted protocol for assessing a patient's brain function after a severe brain injury includes an extensive neurologic exam to assess basic reflexive brain activity and an apnea test, along with arterial blood gases (ABG) performed before and after the apnea test. The apnea test is a breathing test (or a lack-of-breathing test, by definition) performed by temporarily disconnecting the ventilator from the patient and allowing them to attempt to breath on their own. If the brain injury is severe enough to cause cessation of the respiratory drive, the CO_2 level in the blood stream will rise to toxic levels. If no respiratory effort is observed from the patient and the ABG performed after the apnea test shows a significant increase in serum CO_2, then the test is considered positive which indicates an extremely poor prognosis for the patient; no meaningful hope for recovery – death without artificial life support.

Dr. Childers picks up the chart from the table in front of him, opens it and flips through the tabs to find the lab results section. He carefully reviews the report and comments, "Look at that elevated CO_2 level." In a hopeful tone he asks Courtney, "Were you present during the apnea test?"

"Yes sir, I was."

"Did you observe any respiratory effort at all?"

"No sir, none."

"Okay then, that confirms it," he says as he turns and gazes into JT's room at Loretta and her family.

He slowly closes the chart and sets it back on the desk.

141

He sullenly reports aloud, "This young man is brain dead."

A calm silence falls over them. As in life, activity around them continues. But, within the confines of that tight little table area, the two of them share a moment of veneration for JT, his family and the loss that the medical team feels with each bad outcome.

Courtney attempts to provide some support by saying, "I'm so sorry Dr. Childers. We did all we could."

"I know we did, it's not that. It's difficult to lose any patient, but more so under these circumstances; a young man with so much potential."

"Yes, we can all understand that."

Dr. Childers, standing in silence, removes his glasses and rubs his forehead; clearly wrestling with emotion and fatigue. He places his glasses back on and regains his composure. He asks, "Did anyone reach the MDN folks yet?"

"Yes, Jennifer made the referral and I was told in report that their team is on their way."

"Very well." Solemnly, he continues, "Courtney, can you please find me an available consultation room so I can talk to the family in private before their team arrives?"

"I will," she says.

"I'll need a few minutes to collect my thoughts." In a rare moment of weakness, he confides in Courtney, "This is the worst part of my job and I truly wish I were better at it."

Just as Dr. Childers walks away, Kevin and Melanie Precissi approach the Nurse's Station. Melanie is a motherly-type woman who's short in stature but long on heart. She's in her early fifties and has a has an extremely trustworthy appearance; perfectly suited for her role as a Family Support Liaison.

The Missouri Donor Network has compiled her team of specially trained people from various professions including, nursing, pastoral care and social work whose sole purpose is to help guide the donor families through the process of organ donation; from consent to after care - their support continues for years after the donation takes place. Melanie's background in Social Work has prepared her well for the support that she provides to these grieving, vulnerable and confused families. She, herself, was affected by organ donation with the sudden death of her young niece seven years earlier. After a tragic playground accident, Melanie's sister agreed to donate her daughter's organs and tissues. The experience changed Melanie's life and she was compelled to get involved, first by volunteering then by bringing her talents to the team at MDN.

The duo of Kevin and Melanie, an Organ Procurement Coordinator and a Family Support Liaison, are an intentionally paired team based on extensive outcome based research. They are there to provide specialized coordinated care for the potential organ donor and their family. In Melanie's seven-year history with MDN, she has sharply developed her skill set and has one of the best consent rates in the region; nearly ninety-three percent of families she works with ultimately consent to donation.

As the MDN team enters the Nursing Station, Courtney approaches them and says, "Perfect timing. I was just telling Dr. Childers that we should be expecting you guys soon."

Kevin responds, as their paths meet, "It's always good to see you, Courtney." Kevin gets right down to business by saying, "Melanie has briefed me, any updates?"

Courtney's cordial tone changes to that of a professional practitioner about to give a formal report. She replies, "Dr. Childers just reviewed all the testing and has officially declared him brain dead. Everything, including his note, is right there in the chart."

"I'm sorry it ended that way, for everyone involved," Kevin sincerely says.

"Dr. C seems to be taking this one hard, he almost seemed upset," Courtney said.

"He's a good guy; misunderstood by many people."

"I agree," Courtney added. "I was just about to put the family in our consultation room so he could give them the news. Loretta, the patient's Mom, is really struggling."

Melanie recognized the mention of JT's family as an opportunity to join the conversation. She said, "Has anyone mentioned organ…"

Kevin, puzzled by the familiarity of the name, interrupts his colleague, "Wait, excuse me Melanie. Courtney, did you just say the patient's Mother's name is Loretta?"

"Yes, why," Courtney replied.

Kevin's confusion continues as he asks for clarity, "What's his name again?"

"James Stone. Well, his family has been calling him JT."

Hearing another familiar name, his look of confusion turns to concern and his verbal tone changes to one of soft sadness. Hoping his understanding is flawed, he seeks confirmation again by asking, "JT is the patient, Loretta is the Mom and they live here in St. Louis?"

Courtney is now alarmed and a bit confused herself. She asks, "Yes, why? What's wrong, Kevin?"

"What room are they in?"

"Twenty-six-Twenty-seven, right over there."

Kevin despondently begins to explain, "I think…". He pauses to convince himself of the possibility, then he continues, "I think I know them. Well, I know her." He begins to walk toward the room and stops himself. He turns back and rejoins the group. Kevin continues, "I need to think

145

about this before I go see her."

"How do you know her? Are you close, sweetie," Melanie asks.

Kevin shakes his head in disbelief, "No, I wouldn't say we're close, but we are friends. She works at the City Forum Diner, by the office. She must be devastated; he was about to go play pro basketball."

Courtney adds, "Yes, we heard about that. It certainly makes this situation even worse."

"Courtney, is there somewhere we could go, out of sight," Melanie asks.

"Our break room is right over there. You're welcome to go in there."

"Thank you, dear."

Courtney continues, "I'll be back. I need to go help Dr. Childers. Breaking this to them won't be easy, on anyone."

The small group separates. Courtney walks toward JT's room while Kevin and Melanie walk through the door behind the Nurse's Station labeled STAFF ROOM. They enter the room and Kevin immediately leans against the wall. His fingers are interlocked and he nervously spins his wedding ring around on his finger.

Melanie asks, "Are you okay?"

"Yeah, I just don't want Loretta to see me here until the time is right. She knows what I do for a living."

Melanie verbalizes her actual questions, "No, that's not what I meant. Are you going to be okay working on this case? Do we need to make some other arrangements?"

"Ethically, it'll be fine but it won't be easy, emotionally," he replied.

"I've not seen you like this before, sweetie."

"I'll be fine. I just have a lot on my mind," he says as he continues to twist his ring.

Melanie suggests an alternative viewpoint, "You know, your pre-existing relationship may even help."

"We won't worry about that until we get consent."

She asks, "Do you want to come with me when we discuss it?"

"No, let's stick to the process. I don't want her consent to donate to be about me or because of our friendship."

Like the ring on his finger, thoughts are spinning in Kevin's head related to it. Feeling overwhelmed, he announces, "I need to go for a walk and clear my head. Page me if you need me."

CHAPTER 18

Dr. Childers stands just outside the door to the ICU consultation room collecting his thoughts. He must select his words wisely. Although he is no stranger to this type of conversation, he knows this time is different; this is the mother of a teenaged superstar who was destined for great things. He knocks softly on the door and it eases open. As he pushes the door open further, he hears Tanya say, "Come in." The doctor enters the room and takes the empty chair next to the trio on the couch. Courtney occupies the other remaining chair in the room.

Loretta and her family sit patiently waiting to hear why JT's surgeon has called them away from the bedside. Loretta is trying to maintain her outward strength, but inside she fears the worst.

After taking in a slow deep breath, Dr. Childers begins, "Ms. Stone, of all the things that I do on a daily basis, this is by far the most difficult." He pulls in another cleansing breath, then continues. "Unfortunately, despite all our best efforts and using every technology we have at our disposal, we've not been able to save your son. He has not survived his injuries. I'm sorry, Ms. Stone, JT is brain dead."

Loretta bows her head and begins to sob, uncontrollably. Tanya pulls Mikey onto her lap and, together, they embrace Loretta. Dr. Childers continues talking to the shattered family but all that is heard are muffled words as they are deafened by their grief. After what felt like an eternity for the physician, watching the impact and the reality of his words play out in front of him, Loretta finally raises her head. She begins to hear a semblance of his words again. In an effort to ensure her understanding, Dr. Childers asks, "Ms. Stone, do you understand everything I've just told you?"

"Actually, no. No, I don't. How can he be—," Loretta chokes on the word. "How can my boy be dead if his skin is warm, I can see him breathing and I can see his heartbeat on that monitor?"

Dr. Childers answers in a careful compassionate voice, "That's a very good question. You see, all of JT's bodily functions are now supported artificially; his breathing, his heart, everything. If we stopped the breathing machine and the drugs used to support his heart all of his bodily functions would stop within minutes. I am so very sorry, but it's his brain, it's stopped working."

The sounds of intense grief fill the room. Courtney offers a box of tissues to Loretta and Tanya. Mikey sits between the two tearful women with tears in his own eyes.

He has a look of confusion and shock. Loretta leans forward, with her elbows on her knees, in an effort to get closer to the doctor. She pleads for an answer, "Why couldn't you save him? What am I supposed to do now? What about our future?"

Dr. Childers lowers his head, reflecting on the statement that he's about to make, assuring himself of his words. With wet eyes, on the brink of overflow, he tells her, "I am truly sorry, Ms. Stone. We did everything we could." Fearing that he may break down from his own emotions, the doctor stands before them and says, "Courtney will be able to reach me if you have any further questions. I'm terribly sorry for your loss." He, then, somberly exits the room.

Loretta collapses back into the couch from the weight of the moment. Mikey turns and gives his Mother a tight but brief hug. As he pulls away from her she delicately puts her hands on his cheeks, looks directly into his eyes and confirms the news for him, "He's gone, JT's gone." Mikey squeezes his Mother securely again. His understanding catches up with the others, his brother is not coming back.

Loretta releases her hold on her youngest boy and turns to Courtney for some guidance. She asks her, "So, what are we supposed to do now?"

"There's someone here to speak with you about what's next. Is it okay if she comes in to talk with you now?"

Loretta replies, "Yes, but can you please give us a few minutes?"

"Sure. I'll let her know. Her name is Melanie, she's a real sweetheart." In unison, Loretta and Tanya verbalize their appreciation as Courtney stands and exits the room.

Courtney enters the hallway and begins to make her way back to the ICU. Off in the distance, in the shadows of the darkened hallway, Dr. Childers can be seen walking alone. His arms are dangling at his side, in defeat. He stops and leans his back against the wall and drops his head. Although his tears aren't seen, his trembling shoulders reveal his emotional release.

CHAPTER 19

Kevin Mills is well-known for his ability to handle the pressure of his job. He's the senior Organ Procurement Coordinator at MDN, with four years under his belt. This is a job that has a high turn-over rate due to what most coordinators refer to as "beeper anxiety". The average life span for a coordinator is just north of three years. However, the anxiety that he feels for this case is something new for him. Perhaps, if it weren't for the experience he has, he would have folded up under the pressure of knowing the potential donor family. These are uncharted waters.

His angst is evident by the rapid rate of his visible breath in the cold winter air as he paces back and forth around the front entrance to the hospital. He checks his phone and stares at the unanswered text he sent to Sherry just a few minutes prior. "Now a good time to talk," he reads aloud, for the seventh time. His pacing back and forth has gained the attention of the smokers hanging out in "their area". He looks a bit out of place to them without a cigarette in his hand. So not to draw any more attention to himself, he takes a seat on a bench near the door. Just as he sits, he hears that familiar ringtone assigned to his wife. He springs back to his feet and quickly answers the ringing phone.

Sherry is calling from the comfort of her parent's customized, gourmet-style kitchen. She decided to take the afternoon off from work in hopeful anticipation of finally getting to see her husband. She sits at the kitchen table in fashionable Lululemon work-out gear. Beautiful as ever; her hair and her make-up are perfect. Obviously, a workout at the gym isn't the reason for her appearance. Sherry's reasoning for leaving him is valid and her stern position has merit, but she still loves her husband dearly. Their recent hiatus has confirmed that and her Mother's advice has resonated with her.

Answering the phone, Kevin enthusiastically says, "Hello, Sher."

"Hi Kevin. I got your message," she replies.

Reluctantly, Kevin begins to break the news to her, "Yeah, I'm really sorry, but it looks like I won't make it today. Please don't be mad."

The sadness in her voice is apparent, "And, I was really looking forward to seeing you. See, just more disappointment. I will always come second and I wouldn't want our kids to feel this way."

"Come on, please. Like I said in my message, I'm working on something to change all of this."

"Broken record," she fires back.

He continues, trying hard not to take the bait, "Listen,

I'm still down here at University and probably about to start a case that will be extremely difficult for me. Remember that donor case I did last summer; the one with that young girl?"

"Yeah, I know that one really got to you."

"Well, this one could be just as bad, possibly worse."

"Why this one," she asked.

"I happen to know this family. It's tragic."

Sarcastically, she says, "They're all tragic. That's why I can't understand how you do it."

"Sherry, there's something about the opportunity I have to try to help make something positive out of something so negative. I know it's hard to understand unless you see it for yourself. It's a moment when people are at their lowest; grief stricken, most exposed and vulnerable. It amazes me every time when the donor family can think of the needs of others. It reaffirms my faith in humanity, that we're all innately good despite what is splattered on the news every night. It's an opportunity that I've been given to change lives."

"I do get that. But, at what cost," she asks.

Kevin pauses to consider her question, then he says, "Just don't give up, please."

"I don't want to give up, but something's gotta give. I'm willing to sacrifice but you're not. I can't go on like this."

"I'm sorry, Sherry. I'll call you when I finish up. Can I come and see you then?"

"Please call first, since we both know that you have no idea what time of the day or night it might be." Her frustration is apparent in her response.

Message received.

"I will," he responds. Kevin quickly changes to a lighter subject by asking, "By the way, how was the girl's weekend?

"It was nice, except I had to listen to my sister go on about being pregnant. And, believe it or not, my mother is sticking up for you."

A surprised grin fills his face. He says, "Wow! I'll be sure to thank her."

An awkward silence develops as neither of them really want to hang up the phone but realize the conversation is over. Sherry, spurts out, "Well, I guess I'll actually go to the gym since I'm dressed for it."

His eyes brighten with joy as he recalls what that image looks like, he replies, "Oh man, I love when you wear that I-like-to-look-like-I-go-to-the-gym look."

Sherry giggles and in a flirty voice, she responds, "I know, that's why I'm wearing it."

"That gives me hope." Recalling his current duties, Kevin says, "I better get going. But, please know that I can't wait to see you."

There is silence on Sherry's part as she is wrestling with her emotions. She wants to keep her wall up, but can feel it crumbling. Kevin continues, "Sherry, I love you." He pauses before hanging up and closes his eyes in hopeful anticipation, waiting for a response.

After, seemingly forever, Kevin hears the words for which he's been waiting. She replies, "I love you too. Good luck on your case."

"Thanks, baby. You just made my day."

CHAPTER 20

A knock on the door to the ICU consultation room interrupts the conversation between the sisters and Mikey. Courtney peeks her head through the half-opened door and says, "Would it be okay if we come in now?"

Loretta replies, "Yes, come on in." She stands to greet the two ladies, wiping her eyes dry with a balled-up wad of shredded tissue.

Courtney, cordially begins, "Please let me introduce you to Melanie Precissi. She is a Family Support Liaison with an organization called Missouri Donor Network. This is the woman I was telling you about."

Melanie extends her hand to each of the women and Mikey, saying, "Loretta, Tanya, and Mikey, it's my pleasure to get to meet you all." Turning to acknowledge Courtney, she says, "And, thank you, sweetie, for allowing me the opportunity to speak to them."

Courtney replies, "If anyone needs anything from me, I'll be back in the ICU." She slips out of the room to allow for their privacy regarding this extremely personal and sensitive subject.

Loretta sits back down and Melanie takes the open chair next to her. She asks, "Melanie, is it? What can we do for you?"

"Well, dear, as Courtney said, I'm with Missouri Donor Network. Our organization helps facilitate the process of organ donation for those families who wish to donate their loved one's organs."

Taken a bit off-guard and confused by her statement, Loretta exclaims, "Wait! Are you suggesting that we give you my son's organs?"

"Donation for transplant is an option for you at this point, yes. I am here, along with one of our Organ Procurement Coordinators, to give you information so that you can consider…"

Loretta launches herself out of her chair. Her grief takes over and spills out as aggression. She interrupts Melanie in mid-sentence, "Are you kidding right now? I can't even believe that he's gone and you want me to turn him over to you? I'm not ready for that!"

Melanie retorts in a calming tone of voice, "Ms. Stone, there is no way I can begin to understand what you're going through because I have never sat in that chair. But I do appreciate your position. If I could leave this…"

Loretta cries out, "I'm sorry, but I can't talk about this right now! A mother is not supposed to bury her son! Do you get that?" Loretta begins pacing around the small room.

Tanya and Mikey sit passively, almost afraid to interject for fear of being lashed out upon.

"I completely understand." Placing some literature on the small table in front of the couch, Melanie continues, "I'll leave this information with you, perhaps we can discuss it a little later."

Tanya sees an opportunity to intervene and break the tension that her sister has boiling over. She says in a comforting voice, "Yes, please do. We'll let you know when we're ready. Thank you."

"No, thank you for your time and please accept my condolences on behalf of MDN." Melanie quickly stands and exits the room. There is no warmth for her in there.

Tanya continues to try to pacify the situation. She pats the empty seat next to her on the couch. "Loretta, please sit down. That lady didn't do or say anything to deserve that."

"Whose side are you on here?"

Tanya, trying to back-pedal a bit says, "I know you're upset. I'm just trying to…"

Loretta cuts her off quickly, "Trying to help? Is that what you're gonna say?"

In a de-escalating tone, she continues, "Yeah, to help you through this."

Loretta realizes her misplaced aggression. She walks toward the couch and collapses into the seat next to Tanya and says, "I know. I just can't believe he's gone, just like that. I'm so confused. I don't know why this is happening to us."

Tanya puts her arm around Loretta's shoulders. "Sis, sometimes it's hard to see the answers right away. As much as we demand to know why, it takes time to recognize the truth, to find it."

"You're right, and I'm sorry. Maybe the answer is under a rock that I'm not willing to turn over," Loretta confesses.

They embrace, in an effort to ease the pain.

"Give it time, Lo. The answers will come. God has a plan for us all."

Loretta breaks their hug and secretly acknowledges the fact that her level of control is limited, something to which she is not accustomed. She says, "Maybe that's what I need, some Divine guidance."

"You know, there's a chapel by the front lobby?"

Loretta pauses to consider the possibility of allowing God to help guide her upcoming decisions. Her spiritual relationship with God has been strained since her husband died and Loretta didn't have much faith left. Realizing that this may be an opportunity to change that, she said to Tanya, "Would you mind if I..."

With an approving smile, Tanya interrupts her, "Go ahead. I'll look after Mikey."

The threesome gathered up their belongings, with Loretta retrieving the MDN literature from the table. She took a long look at it, as if staring through it. Without saying a word, she brought the brochures to her chest, closer to her heart, desperately looking for an answer.

CHAPTER 21

The University Hospital Chapel is more of an oversized reflection room than it is a formal House of God. For family members, it's a non-denominational escape from the stresses of ill or injured loved ones. It's also an oasis for the weariest of healthcare workers in need of a spiritual respite.

The chamber offers no pulpit, no altar. The only symbol of Christianity is a large wooden cross that hangs from the vaulted ceiling in the front of the room. It's illuminated from the front, artfully casting intentional shadows on the white bare walls behind it. It's a true work of art commissioned by the hospital. The artist ended up donating his work on behalf of Dr. Barkley Childers. The artist's wife was the unfortunate victim of a brain tumor. After reduction with chemotherapy agents and radiation therapy, the tumor was skillfully resected for cure. Her life is just one of the many lives Dr. Childers has been credited with saving.

Loretta is seated in the second to last row of benches along the far-right wall. She is quietly crying. It's been six years since she's seen the inside of anything that resembled a chapel; the funeral for her husband was the direct result of that. She appears uncomfortable with the room and the empty silence within it as she stares into her lap and nervously shreds her tear-filled tissue.

A lone woman, kneeling on the ground in the front row of benches, inaudibly talking to herself catches Loretta's attention. Her curiosity gets the best of her and she relocates herself to the left side of the chapel, almost halfway toward the front. Now within earshot, Loretta is able to make out what the woman is saying. She recognizes her words as The Lord's Prayer, followed by several Hail Mary prayers in a row. "She's saying the Rosary," Loretta whispers to herself. At that moment, Loretta looks up and notices the shadows being cast on the wall in front of the chapel. This was not obvious to her from the back of the room. She perceives the beauty and begins to wonder if the artwork is the cross itself or is it actually the shadows cast by the light. "What could that mean," she ponders.

One of the beautiful things about art is the individual interpretation that each observer can glean from it. For Loretta, she decided, the art was not the cross itself, but rather, the shadows on the wall. In her mind, this represents the path that can be illuminated if one allows the "Light" to shine. She recognized the lights hanging from the ceiling as God's Light, herself as the cross and the artful shadows as her path to a beautiful future. It was at that moment that Loretta decided to allow her decisions regarding JT, her family, and her future to be guided by a "Higher Power," as she preferred to call it. A peaceful calm came over her and she knew that was the right thing to do.

After about thirty minutes, the woman from the front row stood up and began to exit the chapel. Loretta surreptitiously followed her movements as she walked past her. The woman wasn't crying, as Loretta expected. Instead, she seemed at peace. Loretta turned her head and watched as the woman exited. She was then able to notice that she was now alone in the room. Loretta stands and begins to make her way to the very front, where she could examine the cross more closely. The nearer she gets, she's able to see the minor imperfections along the edges of the wood. This closer vantage point also allows her to see the shadows in more detail. These imperfections were readily seen in the shadows as well when close up. After considering the meaning, she concluded that, such as life, nothing is perfect. This insight has given Loretta inspiration and hope. "I am far from perfect and I know I've made mistakes, but I know that with help I can have a bright future," she proudly announced. Her tears have subsided.

Loretta drops to a kneeling position, closer to and underneath the hanging cross. Her hands are folded in a prayerful manner and her head is pressed against them. Her mouth moves silently. She lifts her head to the heavens as a comforting smile appears on her tired face.

CHAPTER 22

Loretta and Tanya stand arm-in-arm, peering through the open door to JT's room. They watch as Courtney attends to his personal needs, just as a mother would for her sick child. JT's outward appearance has not changed. In fact, if anything, things inside the room have become eerily calm. Most often, the diagnosis of brain death brings an end to all the wild vital sign changes and hemodynamic instability that occurs when the brain is fighting for its existence. All the therapies that are keeping his body alive continue until the family is ready to make those end-of-life decisions; the medications continue to flow and the ventilator continues to breathe for him, for now.

Courtney, while using an overhead lift device to adjust JT's position in bed, notices the two women standing in the doorway. She offers, "Feel free to come on in. I'm just turning him, I want to make sure he's comfortable." Courtney knows that he feels no more pain or discomfort because of the severity of his brain injury, but she also knows that treating the family is just as important to her. Making sure that the family knows that JT's care doesn't end with that horrible diagnosis will go a long way in treating the family's pain of loss, and Courtney is one of the best there is.

Loretta walks through the door and into the room. As she approaches her son's bedside, she says, "Thank you, Courtney, for all that you have done for us. You and the night nurses have been wonderful."

"You don't owe me any thanks." Courtney takes a long gaze at Loretta's shirt and asks, "I've noticed that jersey you have on, is that JT's?"

"Oh my, yes. I forgot I was wearing it. I always wear one of his jerseys to his games." With a brief hesitation, Loretta pulls the basketball jersey over her head. She leans over the bed and spreads it out over JT's chest. "It belongs to him, is this okay," she asked.

Unexpectedly, the gesture hit Courtney hard and tears begin to well up in her eyes. Working in such an emotionally driven place such as the ICU, she has become a bit immune to things like that. But, that act found a weakness within her tough demeanor. "Absolutely," Courtney replied, then she quickly made her way out of the room before her emotions could, noticeably, spill over.

A long silence takes over the room.

Loretta, after smoothing out the jersey across his chest, turns to Tanya and says, "Tanya, you want to help, so tell me, what do you think JT would want me to do?"

"That's the real question here. It's not our will to be done, it's his," Tanya replies.

Loretta quickly nods her head in agreement, thinking Tanya is referring to God, given her recent pious experience.

Tanya continues, "What would JT want?"

With a look of surprise on her face, Loretta considers this last question. She says, "Well, we never really talked about organ donation, it was never on our radar."

From outside the room, standing in the doorway, Melanie joins the conversation by saying, "I happen to know the answer to that question." She takes a few steps into the room holding a piece of paper in her hand bearing the State Seal of Missouri. She continues, "I came in here to talk to you about that very subject."

Tanya interjects, "How could you possibly know the answer to that?"

"When JT got his driver's license last summer, he was asked if he wanted to be an organ donor. This document from the Missouri Organ Donor Registry confirms that was his wish."

Loretta and Tanya look at each other as if they'd just seen a ghost. Tanya, surprised by the timing of Melanie's disclosure, says, "How about that, Lo?"

Loretta, taking the document from Melanie, proudly looks down at her son then focuses her attention back on the conversation at hand. She admits, "Well, that rock just got flipped." With hesitation in her voice, she continues, "I'm still not sure about this. None of it seems real to me."

"Would it help to have you talk to my colleague from MDN," Melanie asks. "He's the Organ Procurement Coordinator, the clinical expert. He may be able to help you understand better."

Loretta looks toward Tanya and shoots her a wink, and replies, "Sure, why not? Let's turn over a few more rocks."

Tanya turns to Melanie and asks, "If JT already said yes to donation on his driver's license, then why do you need Loretta's consent?"

"Technically, and legally, we don't. But, we, at MDN, feel it's important to involve the designated donor's family in the consent decision. In some isolated cases of complete family opposition, we have not honored the potential donors wishes to be an organ donor. And in those cases, everyone has lost; the family has lost their loved one, the designated donor has lost his or her right and desire to help save lives and those potential organ recipients have lost that chance to live on. So, in those cases, we work with the family members to help them understand so that we may achieve the best outcome, trying to honor everyone's wishes."

Tanya says, "That makes perfect sense, thanks for explaining that."

As Melanie begins to move toward the door, Loretta grabs her attention by saying, "Listen, Melanie, I owe you an apology. I shouldn't have lashed out like that, before."

Melanie turns to face Loretta. Waving off her comment, she says, "Oh, sweetie, please don't even give it another thought. I'll be right back with my partner."

With a new-found enthusiasm, Melanie barges into the nurse's break room to find Kevin packing up his belongings. "Hey, where are you going," she asks.

"I'm going to see my wife. If Loretta's not on board with this, I'd rather she not even know I was here."

"Well, hang on a second. I think I've had a breakthrough with her. You see, JT has already declared himself a donor. Amy found his name on the Donor Registry and faxed the document here."

"Really? Nice work, Mel."

"Yup, I showed her the enrollment form. But, they need some clarification and I think it would be better coming from you. I explained to them what donor designation is and that we are still requesting Loretta's consent."

Smugly, Kevin says, "Okay, I guess it's go-time." He looks at Melanie and sincerely adds, "I knew you were the right person for the job."

In a teasing voice, she replies "Oh really, that must be why you're packing your bags."

Kevin laughs, and a with a bit of embarrassment he says, "You got me on that one. Are they in his room?"

"Yes. Listen, sweetie, she still doesn't know it's you."

Kevin has not shared the news of his promotion with anyone, not even the person who will benefit from it the most, his wife. He wanted Sherry to be the first to know, but in light of this situation he decides to spill the beans. "This is the first time I've had to discuss this with someone I actually know. And, possibly the last time, period."

"What do you mean?"

Kevin continues with his secret, "You've got to keep this quiet. It's being announced tomorrow, but I've been promoted. This is likely my last case." Privately, what a relief Kevin feels having shared the information and excitement for being able to hear the words leave his lips.

"Congratulations are in order, I suppose," she says. "Nothing like added pressure."

"Tell me about it."

"Are you ready for that," she asks.

"The pressure or the promotion?"

Melanie laughs as Kevin slides his white lab coat on and straightens it on his shoulders. He proudly says, "It's what we do; every donor, every organ, every time."

CHAPTER 23

The MDN duo proudly make their way across the Nurse's Station, toward JT's room. They've made this walk before but this one is very different. As Kevin catches a glimpse of Loretta standing at the bedside, a knot begins to build in his stomach and a wave of nervousness overtakes him when he sees Mikey and Tanya curled up on a chair reading a book. The personal nature of this conversation hits him, like no other has, when he sees the family that will be forever changed by this horrific tragedy.

Melanie and Kevin enter JT's room, virtually unnoticed. Melanie clears her throat as a way of announcing their presence. She begins, "Excuse me, Loretta, this is…"

Loretta glances up and over, toward the door, to see the familiar face of Kevin Mills. An expression of shock appears, followed by relief. She approaches him and opens her arms. Somewhat confused, she asks, "Kevin! What are you doing here?" A warm welcoming hug occurs on her part, it's a much-needed embrace – finally a friendly face that she trusts. His response is more of a professional one.

As the squeeze runs its course, Kevin says, "Loretta, please let me say how sorry I am to hear about this. You have my deepest sympathies."

With his comment, Loretta realizes the real purpose of Kevin's visit. She asks, "Wait a minute, you're here to talk to me about JT?"

"Yes, yes I am. Is that okay with you?"

"Honestly, it's so good to see a familiar face." She continues, "If I'm going to have this conversation, I'm glad it's with you." Her understanding of what he does for a living has finally come full circle.

Kevin added, "I just wish it didn't have to be like this."

A glassy-eyed look appears on Loretta's face as she acknowledges her sister and son. "Kevin, this is my sister, Tanya and JT's little brother, Mikey."

"Hi there, Tanya. Mikey, I've heard so much about you from your Mom." Tanya nods her hello. Mikey, shyly, doesn't respond. Kevin returns his attention to Loretta, "Would you like to step outside the room or are you okay discussing this here?"

"No, here is fine. After all, we are talking about my son."

Kevin slowly walks over to the bedside and acknowledges JT by touching his hand. He says, "I agree, completely."

Loretta recalls her recent trip to the chapel and reminds herself to keep an open mind. Having Kevin there helps, but her former attitude could easily creep back into play. Loretta begins, "Before we start talking about the organs...I need a friend here."

Kevin sincerely replies, "I'm here for you too, don't forget that."

In a sullen, almost embarrassed tone, she admits, "I don't know about all this. I'm just so overwhelmed."

"That's understandable. It's a lot to wrap your head around, even for me sometimes."

"I heard the doctor, but I just can't believe that he's..." The word seems so final to her, she just can bring herself to say it. Loretta continues, "I just want my boy to wake up."

In an assuring voice, he says, "I'll do my best to help you make sense of this." He stops to consider his words in order to provide some semblance of understanding. "Unfortunately, I never got to meet JT. So, can you tell me the one thing about him that expressed his joy for life."

"That's easy, basketball."

"No, no, not that. I mean something personal to him. Something that when you looked at him you knew he was full of life."

Loretta glances at Mikey for a moment, then to JT, admiring her life's work. She looks back at Kevin with a simple smile and says, "His eyes. JT could light up a room with his bright hazel eyes. They're always so full of hope, joy, and life."

Kevin smiles back at her and offers out his hand, inviting her closer to the bedside. She approaches, taking Kevin's hand and picking up JT's hand with the other. "I want to show you something," he softly says to Loretta. "Have you seen his eyes, since the accident?"

"No, I didn't think I could."

"This isn't something I've ever done for a family member before, but I think it's important for you to see and it may help you understand." Kevin reaches over and slides open JT's eyelids, exposing his eyes to her. Loretta peers into the open eyes of her son. His once bright hazel-colored eyes that danced with life are now consumed by the deep black circles of his fixed and dilated pupils. The emptiness within them stuns her. Loretta clutches Kevin's arm and rests her head on him. Her silent tears progress to loud, uncontrolled weeping. Kevin presses JT's eyelids closed and sympathetically places his arm around Loretta.

Struggling through her tears, she says, "Those are not the eyes of my baby. It's like his soul is gone. His body is here, but he's gone."

Tanya steps up next to Loretta and Kevin slides away, toward the door. The sisters embrace, offering comfort for each other's sorrow. "Yes, Lo. Yes, he is," Tanya says to her sister.

Melanie, covertly, catches Kevin's attention and a gives

178

a nod toward the door. She says aloud, "Why don't we give you some time?"

Loretta pulls a tissue from the box on JT's bedside table and dabs her eyes. "You don't have to do that, you're both welcome here."

Sensing an opportunity to introduce the subject of organ donation, Kevin says, "Loretta, can I ask you a question?"

"Yes, of course."

Kevin looks toward Mikey, still sitting quietly in the chair next to JT's bed. He grabs Loretta's hand and begins, "If you can, for a moment, take this situation and set it to the side. Imagine yourself in a different situation where JT, or even Mikey, were so sick and the only thing that would save them was an organ transplant." Adjusting his head, so to make direct eye-contact with Loretta, he continued, "Would you be willing to accept an organ from a total stranger in order to save them?"

Loretta's tears begin to spill over again, down her cheeks. Her legs are weak under the weight of that question. She shuffles over to Mikey's side and runs her fingers through his hair as she considers that scenario. She concedes, "Yes, of course, I would."

Kevin allows his question and her answer to hang in the air, resonating with everyone in the room especially with Loretta herself. Waiting just the perfect amount of time, he continues, "Then, won't you please consider doing that for someone else? Provide them with the gift of life."

Loretta lowers her head and sobs with emotion. Tanya continues to comfort her sister.

Melanie breaks the silence by saying, "We'll give you some time."

In this instant, a matter of seconds, memories of JT's life flash through Loretta's head. She recalls his childhood; playing in the cramped apartment with Mikey, first days of school, attending Sunday church services and family reunions. His adolescence was when he discovered the game he loved, all those practices, games and tournaments. She recalls his teenage years, when he truly grew and showed his true self; JT had a giving soul and showed it readily by making sacrifices for his family, especially after the death of his father. He stepped up, he gave away his adolescence for the betterment of his loved ones. He most recently was ready to delay his goal of playing his game professionally just so his Father's dream of a college education could be attained. Loretta realized that she had raised a selfless young man, "So why stop him now?" she thought quietly to herself.

Loretta returns from her daydream to rejoin her family and friends in that hospital room. She takes a quick moment to look around the room, at her reality. With warmth in her heart and pride in her soul, she drops her head and exclaims,

"No!"

Melanie and Kevin, in unison, drop their heads in defeat. Kevin pleads with her, "Please take some time to consider this."

Loretta raises her head to reveal a smile that has come over her face. She proudly says, "No, I don't need more time. The answer is yes!" Tanya lifts her head toward the heavens and breathes an enormous sigh of relief. Melanie and Kevin drive looks of approval and gratitude toward Loretta. She continues, "The very last thing that JT said to me was that all he wanted was for me to be proud of him." Loretta pauses to catch her breath and wipe away her tears. She continues to explain her rationale, "For him to do this...it's more honorable than anything he could ever do on the basketball court." She breaks into a smile, reveling in the peace within her heart. "The answer is yes," she exclaimed.

Melanie responds out of sheer pride for the job Kevin did explaining the situation and for the consideration Loretta gave to her decision. "Ms. Stone, we know that wasn't easy for you, sweetie. Thank you."

"Dear, you can call me Loretta," she said, smiling through her tears.

"Loretta, why don't you guys come with me and we will take care of a few details. This will allow Kevin some time to work with JT to start his evaluation."

As the group begins to exit the room, Loretta turns to face Kevin with a look of desperation on her face. She says to him, "Please take good care of my boy. I leave him in your hands."

"He'll be treated with the utmost respect and dignity, you can count on that." Kevin takes her hands in his and says, "I am so proud of you for seeing the possibility of good despite all of this tragedy." He paused, momentarily, "JT would be proud of you today."

CHAPTER 24

Kevin has established a nice little workstation in the Neuro ICU; not so little, in fact. His space is tattered with open binders, loose papers, two different open laptop computers, his cell phone and a land line - all spread across the oversized worktable in the Nurse's Station. From a distance, he has the appearance of maestro about to take command of an orchestra, minus the tuxedo and crazy hair. The ICU staff have become accustomed to sharing their workspace with the Missouri Donor Network team, so they don't mind. They realize the importance of the work that will take place in the coming hours.

Inside the same consultation room that the tragic news of JT's death was given by Dr. Childers, JT's family is beginning the process of donation by completing the required paperwork to allow the endowment of JT's organs to take place. While Kevin begins JT's clinical evaluation in the Neuro ICU, Melanie is with the family, every step of the way, explaining the details of the documents and the nuances that they may encounter along the way. The first document is the consent form itself. In signing this document, Loretta willfully agrees to full consent, granting the wish that JT had to be a full organ donor. He is eligible to donate his heart, lungs, liver, kidneys, pancreas and small intestine for life-saving transplant. In addition, she has permitted the procurement of JT's tissues; corneas, tendons, heart valves (not used for organ transplant), veins, skin and bones. The tissues can be used to enhance the lives of up to fifty different people.

The next document that Melanie will complete with Loretta is the Medical and Social History Questionnaire. This document is required to obtain as much information about the donor as possible. The information will be used by the recipient transplant surgeons to make decisions about the quality and match of the donor organ to their recipient. Some of the information gathered with this document is a bit sensitive in nature, such as, increased risk behaviors of the donor like the use of intravenous drugs, homosexual activity, sex with others for drugs or money. While intrusive, this information is vital in determining the possibility of transferring communicable diseases from donor to recipient by way of organ transplant. It's all about minimizing risk of exposure to the recipient. Organs from donors that are considered increased risk can still be used for donation as long as the risk of transmission doesn't outweigh the benefit of the transplant.

After completing all the required documentation and having their appropriate questions addressed, Melanie leads the family out of the consultation room and back toward the ICU. As the group enters the unit, they pass Kevin sitting at his workstation. He looks up from his business as they pass. "How did everything go, Loretta," he asked. Melanie and Loretta stop to chat with Kevin while Tanya and Mikey continue on to JT's room.

"You guys sure do get personal, don't you," Loretta said.

"Oh, you must be talking about the medical and social history questionnaires. Well, I'm sure Melanie told you why those intrusive questions are important."

Loretta responds in a defensive tone, "Yeah, she did. But, my boy was not into drugs or sex for money or any of those types of behaviors that she asked about."

Melanie jumps in to de-escalate the topic, "Nope, no surprises at all. We had a feeling that there wouldn't be any problems with the questionnaire. But, we still have to ask."

"We have an obligation to the recipients of any organ that we procure to ensure that we know as much about the donor and their lifestyle as possible," Kevin explained.

"Yeah, I understand. I guess I would want to know if I were receiving an organ, so I get it," Loretta said. "So, what's going to happen next," she asked Kevin.

"I'll be right in to tell you what's next. Sound good?"

"Sure, I'll just go into JT's room and wait for you."

Loretta turns to make her way into the ICU room to join her sister and her boys.

Melanie produces two packets of paper and hands them over to Kevin. "Here's the signed Consent Form and the Med-Social Questionnaire. As I said, no surprises."

"Thanks for taking care of that."

"Kevin, you did such a great job with her. Where did that come from?"

Kevin explained, "I guess knowing her like I do did help. I just thought about what she needed to hear to get to that decision."

"We're gonna miss you in the field, that's for sure, sweetie."

"Thanks, but I can't think about that right now. What's before me is the most important thing. This case needs to be flawless, for many reasons."

Kevin enters JT's room to find Loretta watching over her son while Courtney and another nurse tend to his clinical needs. Tanya and Mikey are standing in front of the window playing a game of "I Spy," overlooking the buildings and lighted streets of downtown St. Louis.

"You sure could pass for a doctor," Loretta snickers as she admires Kevin's professional appearance and his heavily starched white lab coat. "So, what happens now," she asks.

"You're too much," he jokingly says. Taking a more serious tone, he explains, "For the next several hours, we'll be performing various tests and procedures to evaluate each of JT's organ systems."

"Like his heart and stuff?"

Kevin replies, "Yes, his heart, his lungs, digestive and kidney function. We will also be testing his blood for various diseases. Like I said before, we need to make sure each transplant is safe to perform."

"I had no idea that there was so much to all of this," Loretta confesses. "Will I be able to stay with him?"

"I've already ordered all the testing that the hospital staff will be doing and fortunately, because of his relatively good health and young age, all of the testing will be done here in his room. So, yes, you guys will be able to be here for most of it."

"Most," she questioned.

"Well, there's one test that I will be doing that you may not want to see. I have to look down into his lungs with a scope to assess anatomy and to retrieve a tissue sample."

Wrinkling up her face, she says, "Yeah, I'll pass on that one." A knocking on the glass door catches them all off guard. It's a young lady dressed in purple scrubs with a large monitoring device on wheels.

"Pardon me, doctor…"

"See, I'm not the only one," Loretta quips.

"Let it go," Kevin says as he laughs out loud.

"Hi, I'm Linda from the Echocardiography Department. Did you order an echo for…," pausing to examine the order sheet in her hand, "James Stone?"

"Yes, I did. Thank you," he replied. "Loretta, she's here to do the evaluation of JT's heart function. It's a non-invasive look at his beating heart to make sure it's healthy."

"On second thought, I think we'll step out. We can get a bite to eat and take a walk," she said.

"That's a great idea," Tanya says as she leads Mikey toward the door.

Kevin joins them as they head out of the room. He offers, "That sounds like a great plan. I will go ahead and do my bronchoscopy right after Linda is done. We'll need about an hour, or so."

"Sounds good, Kevin."

"Before you go, there's another opportunity I want to offer to you, but it's completely optional. We've implemented a new program called A Moment of Silence, it's an opportunity to honor JT in the OR, prior to the surgery."

Loretta replies, "Awe, that sounds so nice."

Kevin continues, "If you'd like, please prepare a short,

written statement that I will read aloud to the procurement team. It's entirely up to you. If you wish to do it, just give me that statement before we go to the OR."

"I'll give it some thought and let you know."

As the family trio head toward the ICU exit doors, Loretta grabs Tanya's hand and says, "Have I thanked you lately for staying here by my side and for helping out with Mikey?"

"No, but you don't need to do that. We're sisters, we will get through all of this together," Tanya replied. "But, I will let you buy me dinner." They both laugh.

For the most part, their tears have been replaced by lightheartedness in an effort to squelch the pain and sorrow they feel inside. For Loretta, this is the execution of the conscious decision made in the chapel a few hours before.

CHAPTER 25

Kevin sits at his makeshift workstation, before his organized chaos; he's evaluating the results, updating transplant surgeons and allocating organs to the neediest of recipients. His focus on this case is razor sharp.

Melanie approaches just as Kevin is getting off the phone. She asks, "How's the evaluation going?"

"Really well. Lab results are steadily coming in and everything looks great. Echo and Bronch are completed, nothing wrong with either," Kevin replies. "In fact, I've placed the heart with the program here at University. I'm getting ready to start the lung allocation next."

"That's great news, Kevin. Have you told Loretta?"

"No. Actually, I haven't seen them in a few hours." A somewhat concerned look appears on his face. He continues, "They left quite a while ago to get some dinner but I haven't seen them return."

"I saw them in the waiting room just a bit ago," she reported.

"Great, I'll go give them an update."

Kevin enters the waiting room to find them sleeping on the couches. A short debate takes place in his head over whether or not to wake them. It is the middle of the night and they sure could use the rest is one argument, but a significant update in the case is the counter-point. After this brief internal struggle, Kevin recalls the words of one of his idols; Albert Einstein, "knowledge is power". With that he decides that information is more important than sleep.

He gently touches Loretta on the shoulder and says, "Loretta, I'm sorry to wake you."

She springs from her slumber and loudly says, "What is it? Everything okay?" Her outburst wakes anyone within ear shot, including Tanya.

Kevin replies, "Yes, everything is fine. I haven't seen you guys since you left for dinner and wanted to give you an update."

Loretta says, "I was back there a little while ago, but I don't think you noticed me."

"I'm sorry, I've been a busy man."

She asks, "How's everything going?"

"Remarkably well. I had a feeling that this might go relatively fast because he's so young and healthy. I was right."

"I bet you're right a lot," Tanya says from the next couch over. "What time is it?"

"It's just after midnight," Kevin replies. "I came out here to let you know that JT is a very popular young man tonight."

"How so," Tanya asks.

"Well, I cannot tell you where or to whom, out of respect for the recipient's privacy, but I have placed his heart already and there is interest in his lungs. I will start working on his abdominal organs after I get something to eat."

"Can I go get you something," Tanya offers.

Loretta adds, "Yes, what would you like, anything at all."

"No ladies, I can't allow you to do that for me, ethically. But, I do appreciate your offer." Kevin says with a wink of his eye, "Now, I wouldn't dare turn down a home-cooked meal in a week or two."

Loretta nods her head and says, "We will definitely make that happen."

"For now, it's cafeteria food for me," Kevin laments.

Tanya asks, "What time do you think the operation will take place?"

"It looks like it will be sometime in the morning. I haven't set that up yet because I still need to allocate the abdominal organs. I don't see that being a problem though. As I said, he is very popular."

Loretta says, "We trust you with everything." She stands up and stretches out her back. "I'm not gonna miss that couch, that's for sure."

"Why don't you go on back and be with JT? I'll stay

here with Mikey, so he can sleep," Tanya offers to Loretta.

"I think I will. Thank you, dear."

Kevin says, "Alright then, I'll be back after I get some food. Hang in there, we've almost got this part finished."

"It's far from over though, isn't it," Loretta asks.

Kevin sincerely replies, "We, especially me, will be with you every step of the way."

A radiology technician arrives at the door to JT's ICU room. He is there to perform a repeat chest x-ray. "Three AM, right on time," Kevin announces. "Now, that's what I call great timing, thank you."

Loretta stirs from her half-sleep in the chair at JT's bedside, "Another test," she asks.

"It's just a quick x-ray that the lung team wants to ensure that there have been no changes," he explains.

"They sure are particular, aren't they?"

"It's just that lungs are very sensitive organs and difficult to place."

"I've been praying for the best possible outcome for everyone involved," Loretta said. "Including you. You haven't gotten any sleep, have you?"

"No, but that's okay. I told you in the diner the other day that my job is tough, but rewarding. It's cases like this that give me that feeling of accomplishment. Helping you through this is definitely worth one sleepless night for me."

"You're such a good man, Kevin."

"Let's step outside while they shoot this x-ray. I have another update for you." The two of them move out into the hallway, clear of the working x-ray machine and its focused radiation. "Allocation is all done," he tells her.

"You've placed his organs?"

"Yes, we're all set to go. We won't be going to the operating room for several more hours. Some of the recipient teams need a little time to prepare for their surgeries, which is normal. Everyone has to be in place and ready at the same time."

"Amazing, just amazing."

"It's a well-orchestrated process to get everything to line-up exactly right," Kevin explained. "Please take the next few hours with your family, together. I will do my best to eliminate interruptions for you."

"We appreciate that, Kevin. We appreciate everything that you have done for us."

He nods his head and walks away before his emotions surface. Being awake for close to twenty-four hours can cause a chink in anyone's armor, and now is not the time to break down. The Stone family is looking to him for strength in the face of their weakness.

CHAPTER 26

The Medical Intensive Care Unit of University Hospital is located on the same floor as the Neuro ICU, but in the opposite wing of the expansive Medical Center. Since being intubated and placed on the ventilator, Bryan Kelley has been moved from the Emergency Department to the high-tech Medical ICU. He's been sedated with IV medications to ensure his comfort and is unable to verbally respond due to the breathing tube in his trachea.

Trina Kelley sits quietly with her legs propped up next to her husband's hospital bed. The room is dark and void of energy as soft music is playing from Bryan's favorite artist, James Taylor. While not on her knees, she is praying for a miracle.

There is a light tapping on the door which causes Trina to spring to attention. The door slowly opens and Dr. Martina Bankston enters. She has been one of Bryan's primary doctors for the last three years, since he was referred for advanced treatment for his chronic lung disease. She, like Dr. Childers, is on staff at University Hospital. She is a well-respected leader and one of only a handful of female transplant surgeons in the country in her field of specialty.

With her thick British accent, she makes her presence

known, "Hello, Trina. May I come in?"

"Yes, of course you can Dr. Bankston. You don't need my permission," she says in a welcoming voice. Concern for more bad news consumes Trina and she nervously asks, "What's wrong?"

"There's nothing wrong at this hour. Only good news," she begins.

"What good news," Trina queries as she scrambles for the bed control to turn on the overhead light.

"Is Bryan awake?"

"Off and on, really. He has no energy," Trina explains.

"This news may help," the doctor teases.

Trina pleads with her for information, "What is it? Please tell me."

Dr. Bankston addresses the ashen-appearing patient and his wife, together. "I just came by to tell you, in person, that we have a potential lung donor for you."

"Are you kidding? That's the most wonderful news!" Trina leans into her husband's ear and gently strokes his cheek. "Did you hear that sweetheart? It's going to happen." Bryan summons the energy to open his eyes and looks up at Trina. Unable to speak, he musters up a bright-eyed nod of approval.

Dr. Bankston touches their interlocked fingers, smiles and says, "Keep up the fight Bryan, just a few more hours."

He closes his eyes, and slides back into his unconscious state.

"A few hours? Can you be more specific," Trina probes.

"All I can tell you is that it's a local donor. So, it may go soon. I'm going to go assess the lungs for myself. That's all I know right now."

"We're so grateful." Joyful tears well up in Trina's eyes as she pulls Dr. Bankston in for an awkward hug.

Trina's exuberance now fills the entire room.

The lung transplant surgeon pulls away from the unwelcome contact and explains what to expect next. She says, "The nurses will be in shortly to start prepping Bryan for surgery. For now, I've got to get going."

"I can't thank you enough!"

"No need for that." Dr. Bankston quickly exits before she gets hugged again.

Trina scurries to collect all of her belongings, but soon realizes that she has nowhere to go. She grabs her phone and notices a missed call displayed on the screen. Aloud, to herself, she declares, "Shoot, I missed a call from Loretta. I've got to tell her that our prayers have been answered."

Loretta sits quietly, alone in JT's room, cherishing these last few quiet moments that she has with her son. "The moonlight is especially bright through the window tonight, JT," Loretta describes. The rhythmic sound of the ventilator is the only response that she will get; she knows that now, and has accepted it.

The one-sided conversation ends as a light knocking on the glass door to JT's room is heard. The soft gentle voice of Trina breaks through the silence, "Loretta, are you awake?"

Loretta turns in her chair, like a flower turns toward the sun, to see her best friend standing in the doorway. It's apparent from Loretta's face that she is actively crying as she dabs her eyes with a tissue. "Yes, I'm awake. Come on in, Trina. I'm so happy to see you."

Trina timidly approaches JT's hospital bed. The sight of this young man connected to a ventilator, all the protruding tubes and the IV pumps is disturbing for Trina. She reaches down and touches JT's hand, turns to Loretta and says, "I had no idea – I'm so sorry. I would have been here sooner." She bows her head for a moment of quiet reflection. Trina turns back to Loretta and says, "The nurses told me where to find you." Looking around the room, she asked, "Are you here alone, Lo?"

"Tanya and Mikey went for a walk, he was getting cranky."

With genuine concern, Trina inquires, "Have you eaten anything? Slept at all?"

Loretta replies, "I'll be fine." Abruptly, she says, "I called you."

"Yeah, sorry I missed it. I was using my phone to play music for Bryan." Trina's excitement begins to spill over and she starts explaining, "I've got the most wonderful news."

Loretta, unable to contain her grief, stands up and begins sobbing uncontrollably. She interrupts her friend, "He's gone Trina, my JT is gone."

Trina grabs Loretta's arm in an effort to help keep her upright and guides her back to her chair. "What do you mean, gone?"

"He was hurt too badly and they weren't able to save him. He's brain dead."

Trina turns toward JT with a horrified look on her face and gasps. She turns back to face her best friend again and suddenly forgets the reason for her visit. She kneels on the ground in front of Loretta and allows her to empty her emotions onto her shoulder. After a few long moments of grieving pass, Trina asks, "So, what happens now?"

Loretta explains, through her tears, "I've agreed to donate JT's organs."

Hearing these words echo around the room sends a jolt through Trina and she abruptly recalls why she's there; to share her news. She grabs Loretta's arms and gently pushes her away, to her arms-length and says, "Lo, that's amazing."

Trina immediately begins calculating the possibility in her mind.

Loretta begins telling her story, "Yes, I wasn't too sure about it at first."

As Loretta tries to explain, Trina stands and takes a step back away from her. She interjects, "Wait, Lo. I've got to tell you something."

A bit annoyed by the interruption, Loretta snaps, "What?"

"It can't be," Trina mumbles as she is still trying to calculate the possibility.

"What, what is it?"

Trina just blurts it out. "Bryan was just offered a lung transplant. He's being prepped for surgery right now."

"That's fantastic," Loretta exclaims.

"But, our surgeon said they are from a local donor," Trina says in a leading tone of voice. The logic catches up with Loretta as a look of shock washes over her face. Trina continues, "Lo, do you think it's possible?" They hold hands and stare directly into each other's eyes. Trina finally verbalizes the question that they both are wondering, "After fourteen months of waiting, is Bryan being offered JT's lungs?"

Loretta breaks the contact and walks slowly toward the picture window. After an eternity of silence, Loretta says,

"Well, it does makes sense. They're similar in size, and the timing...it just can't be a coincidence."

"I'm so happy and so sad at the same time, Trina admits. "I don't know what to feel."

"I've been here thinking about this for hours, ever since I consented to the donation." Loretta turns back in the direction of Trina and begins walking toward her as she explains. "I may never fully understand why, but I've accepted the fact that JT is gone. He's gone way too early, but, this is his opportunity to leave a mark on this world." She takes a brief moment to dry the tears from her eyes and cheeks. Standing before Trina, face-to-face, she continues, "I've thought about the people that are going to get his organs, how their lives and the lives of their families are going to be changed, forever." She begins to smile at her dear friend and she grabs her hands, again. "It gives me peace to know that one of them might be you."

With tears in her eyes, Trina wraps her arms around Loretta and they weep, together, for the simultaneously worst and best moments in their lives. Trina whispers into Loretta's ear, "Thank you, Sweetie. Bryan and I are eternally grateful."

CHAPTER 27

The ICU room continues to be kept dimly lit, not because it needs to be any longer but rather that's how Loretta has wanted it. It's almost cathartic for her. In a way, she feels closer to her son who will no longer see the light of day. She sits quietly next to his bed reading from a hand-written piece of paper. She smiles proudly, with pen in hand, dotting her "I's" and crossing her "T's". She, then, folds the paper in half and stuffs it into her purse.

Kevin knocks on the door and quietly enters JT's room. Loretta is seated next to JT's bed; her head is near his hand on the mattress. She's not quite asleep, but resting her eyes as she daydreams of happier days. Tanya and Mikey sit quietly together on a bedside chair playing with one of Mikey's action figures.

"May I turn the light on, Loretta," Kevin asks.

"Yes, go ahead." She lifts her head from the bed surface and stretches out her stiff back. She asks, "How are things going? Any updates?"

Kevin gently touches Loretta's shoulder. He softly says, "We are just about ready to get JT to the operating room. The surgical teams are on their way here now."

Tanya wrestles her way out of the chair and asks, "How much more time do we have?"

"We'll need to get going very soon. I tried not to disturb you guys until it was absolutely necessary," he explained to them.

"Okay, I understand," Loretta said.

Kevin addresses the group, "We'll give you guys a few moments alone with him, then we have to go." Kevin willfully withdraws himself from the room, he's seen this scene all too many times.

Loretta holds out her hand to Mikey and invites him to come closer. She says, "Mikey, come say goodbye to your brother."

Mikey, with obvious apprehension, approaches his mother and says, "I don't know what to say Mommy. I'm going to miss him, I know that. He's my big brother." He elects to, instead, bury his head behind Loretta's back; once again, hiding his tears.

Tanya approaches JT's bed, leans over and carefully kisses JT on the cheek. She quietly whispers into his ear as she chokes on her emotions, "Your fate here on earth was never guaranteed. Rest well in heaven where you'll always be an all-star." With tears streaming down her face, she continues, "I love you my sweet nephew and will always brag about you and forever celebrate your life."

Tanya grabs Mikey's hand and starts to lead him out of the room. He breaks free of her hold, turns and runs the few steps to his brother's bedside. With tears welling up in his eyes, Mikey touches his brother's arm and leans over to kiss JT's hand. He says, in a loud and proud voice, "I love you, brother!"

Tanya returns and picks Mikey up and gives him a sweet hug. She whispers to him, "I'm so proud of you." Together they exit the room. From over Tanya's shoulder, Mikey looks at his brother one last time as he wipes tears from his face.

Loretta, now alone with her son, takes this opportunity to look around the room. She notices everything; she's hyper-aware of all the details, from the cleanliness of the floors to the contrasting color of white walls and the red electrical outlets behind JT's bed. She sees the stickers on the IV tubing identifying each of the drugs infusing into her son's veins and, as she gazes around the room, she notices a cross on the wall near the door. Until this very moment, she had overlooked that ornament. "He's been here the whole time," she said softly, aloud to herself.

A reassuring, calm peace comes over her as she allows these images to burn into her memory. It's a moment of pride that she wants to remember, forever.

She deliberately approaches her son's bedside and begins

to speak her final words to him, "Here we are again, kid. Just me and you, for the last time." She tenderly picks up JT's lifeless right hand and leans forward to press it to her lips. She raises her head to look at her son's face. Tears fall from her eyes and onto the skin of his arm. In a hushed voice, she continues, "I owe you an apology. I should've listened to you...I should've let you be a kid. I was being selfish. I tried to push you down a path that I chose for you." She lowers her head onto the surface of his hand and continues without raising her head, "You don't even know it my son, but you've set an example for me tonight and given me a whole new perspective. Don't you worry about Mikey and me, we'll be fine. I'm going to do my best to make *you* proud of *me*; to be the best Momma I can for Mikey." Loretta lifts her head and reaches up to put her hand on JT's cheek. She presses on, "Rest well my son. I will love you forever."

Loretta kisses JT's hand and gently places it back on the bed. She pulls two tissues from the box lying on his bed and touches them to her eyes. Then, she reaches over and carefully lifts the jersey off his body and folds it neatly, with the reverence and precision that American Soldiers give to the American Flag. With the jersey draped over her arm, Loretta turns to leave the room and meets Kevin at the door. Before he can say anything, she wraps her arms around him and weeps tears that only a mother who has lost a child could know.

Kevin escorts Loretta from the ICU room. Once clear of the room, out in the hallway, he stops and faces Loretta. He asks, "Have you thought any more about the Moment of Silence letter we talked about before?"

She begins to dig through her purse and removes the folded piece of paper that she stuffed in there earlier. She replies, "Yes, here you go. That was one of the hardest things I've ever written but I'm grateful for the chance to share that message about him with your surgical teams."

He takes the paper from her, folds it again and slides it into the chest pocket of his scrub top. He pats the pocket and says, "I'll be sure it's done. Thank you."

"No, Kevin, thank you."

He continues, "Now, Loretta, we have something for you." Kevin hands Loretta a small box. She opens it to reveal a bronze metal bearing an emblem for donation and an inscription that reads, "GIFT OF LIFE DONOR".

"Oh, it's beautiful," she says as she admires the craftsmanship.

"This is a donor medal that we give to each donor's family as a reminder and a symbol that their loved one is a champion for donation."

"Thank you so much, Kevin."

Fighting through his own emotional response, trying to

keep this professional, Kevin continues, "It may not be an Olympic medal, an NCAA or NBA trophy but please know that we, especially me, are so proud of JT and of you."

Loretta gives Kevin another strong squeeze and he consciously returns the embrace.

CHAPTER 28

The cleanliness of this room is blinding. In the exact center of the room, hanging from the ceiling, are two sets of large round lights; four lights in all. Each are on, illuminating every inch of the operating table that lies beneath. JT's six-foot, six-inch frame perfectly fills this table. He is covered in blankets to keep his body warm. The rhythmic sound of the ventilator can be heard filling his lungs with oxygen every five seconds. There are no windows to the outside world, but it's as bright as daylight inside.

Jamie Kincaid, one of Kevin's fellow organ procurement coordinators, is positioned at the head of the bed. He's intently monitoring every breath given by the ventilator and every beat of JT's heart on the monitor; game face on. Jamie has been with the organization for a little over a year, another one of Kevin's protégés. With youth on his side and a solid head on his shoulders, he's got a shot at being the next "Kevin".

There are two scrub technicians expertly preparing the surgical instruments for use as Kevin enters the operating suite pulling his mask up over his face. His head is covered with a surgical cap. He announces, "The surgeons are starting to arrive. The lung team is coming down the hall now."

Jamie states, "I've got the bronchoscopy equipment here, ready to go for them."

Just then, the door to the operating suite swings open and Dr. Martina Bankston enters the sterile room pulling on her face mask. She surveys the room and jokingly says, "Am I really the first one here?" She is known for running fashionably late. Kevin and his colleagues have started the practice of running on "Bankston time"; asking her to arrive a bit ahead of the other teams, in order to keep their timing perfect. "Do you have my bronchoscope ready," she asks.

"I have it here," Jamie replies.

As she makes her way to the head of the bed, she says, "Very well. Let's take a look then." She takes the scope from Jamie and inspects the bright light source at the distal end. She wipes the tip clean with a piece of sterile gauze and quickly looks at the vital signs monitor. She then asks Jamie to decrease the PEEP setting on the ventilator and begins her exam.

Dr. Bankston inserts the tip of the scope into the one-way adapter at the top of the breathing tube. The lighted tip disappears down the tube. She presses her eye to the scope and begins manipulating the controls so she can visualize the inside of JT's lungs. "Uh huh," she says without stopping

212

her examination. Then, loudly for the entire room to hear in her proper British enunciation, she says, "With whom was I speaking, on the telephone?"

"That was me, Dr. Bankston. I'm Kevin," he nervously replies from across the room.

"Well, let's see what kind of job you did keeping these lungs viable for me."

Kevin is confident in his work, but he knows from experience that it doesn't take much to turn down lungs at the last minute. Near perfection is what Dr. Bankston often requires. He takes in an anxious, deep breath.

It's Tuesday morning, always an extremely busy day for the University Hospital operating room department. Therefore, the waiting room is buzzing with activity.

Loretta is seated at a small round table near the picture window, overlooking the front entrance to the hospital. Trina approaches her with two cups of coffee and takes the seat across from her friend. She slides a cup across the table, in Loretta's direction, and says. "It's not as good as yours, but it's gonna have to do for now."

Loretta gives a quiet laugh, "Thanks sweetie." She continues her gaze at the sun-filled outdoors.

213

Trina attempts some small talk by asking, "Did your sister get Mikey off to school?"

"Oh, no. He just went on home with her. There will be no school for him this week, I've already decided that."

Looking deeply at Loretta's profile, trying to examine her face, Trina says, "You've got to be exhausted, Lo."

"I'll be fine."

Trina decides to address the elephant in the room. She says, "I can't thank you enough for staying here with me during the surgeries."

Loretta turns in her chair to face Trina. "Of course, Dear."

"I'm sure this isn't easy for you."

Loretta replies, "Well, I want to be here for you and for me. I need to know that it all worked out."

Loretta pulls her bag up onto the table and removes the box that Kevin gave to her. She opens it, slides it toward Trina, and says, "Look at this beautiful medal the Organ people gave me."

Trina runs her fingers over the engraving and considers the meaning behind the medal. "It's beautiful, Lo. What a nice gesture."

"Yes, I'll have to think of a way to display it."

"This deserves something really nice." Trina offers, "I can help you, if you want. It will be a nice project for us to do."

The double doors that lead to the operating room area are electrically powered and open inwardly, into the waiting area. Each time these doors swing open, the occupants of this room turn in unison toward the doors hoping to see the familiar face of the surgeon operating on their loved one, desperately seeking news of their respective procedures.

As the two ladies are finishing their cups of coffee, the doors spring open and through them walks Kevin Mills. As he enters the waiting area, he pulls off his surgical cap and makes a failed attempt to fix his messy hair. Visibly searching the busy room, he locates Loretta as she is waiving her hand above her head to grab his attention. When he arrives at her table, he notices the woman sitting with her. He asks, "I have an update, Loretta, can we talk?"

"It's okay. This is my dear friend, Trina."

Kevin tilts his head to the side and points toward Trina, "Oh, from the diner?" The ladies share a secret smile.

Loretta asks, "What's going on?"

Kevin pulls an empty chair up to their table and begins, "The lung transplant surgeon is here and has officially accepted JT's lungs. She said that they are a perfect match!"

Trina gasps loudly.

Loretta reaches across the table and clutches Trina's arm. With sincere joy in her heart, she says, "Oh Trina, I'm so happy for you."

Loretta makes eye contact with Kevin and divulges their assumed secret, "Her husband is getting JT's lungs."

This news takes him off guard, he shakes his head in disbelief. He looks off into the distance, testing his recollection. Kevin points toward Trina again, and says, "Bryan Kelley?"

"The one and only," she replies, through her tears.

A bewildered look crosses Kevin's face, he shakes his head, winks at the two of them and says, "I cannot confirm this, but I can't deny that this universe gets smaller and smaller, every day."

Loretta timidly asks, "Has the surgery started?"

"We're about to. I just wanted to come out to tell you the news." Kevin sits up and proudly announces, "JT has gifted seven of his organs today."

Loretta asks, "Gifted?"

"Yes, sorry, we use that term to describe the act of donation," he explained.

A pride-filled smile appears on her face and she jokes, "He's always been gifted."

Trina grabs her hand and gives it a squeeze, while saying, "And now, in every sense of the word."

Kevin stands up, pulls the surgical cap from his pocket and applies it to his head. "I need to go. I'll be back out in a little while."

As he turns to walk away, Trina says, "Thank you for what you're doing."

"Truly, my pleasure." Kevin turns to leave as the two ladies return to their conversation.

Trina says, "You know, because of this, you and I will be connected, forever."

"Kind of like sisters, in a way," Loretta adds.

With a giggle, Trina says, "Yeah, but we don't really look alike."

Laughing herself, Loretta quips, "No, that's true."

Trina begins to think about the concept a little further, "Not exactly, sisters-in-law, either."

A long pause between them occurs. Then, proudly, Loretta announces, "How about sisters-in-life?"

From across the table, Trina reaches out her hands and Loretta grabs them tightly. She softly says, "I love that, Lo; sisters-in-life, we will be."

CHAPTER 29

Kevin Mills enters the operating theatre to find each of the surgical teams prepping for surgery. The surgeons have scrubbed their hands and arms in sterile fashion and are now being assisted by the OR technicians; one by one they dress for surgery, for the procurement of JT's life-saving organs. Each of the physicians, are masked, gowned and gloved. Their heads and hairlines are concealed by surgical caps, some form fitting and others wearing mesh covers that resemble a shower cap. The collective years of experience among the five doctors that have come to work this day approaches the century mark. Their skills and talents have been honed and perfected over years of dedication to serving others.

Dr. Bankston, there to recover the lungs, has been joined by Dr. Sanji Sandau; he has come to procure the heart for one of his patients. The two are across the table from one another. They will be working in the chest, simultaneously. Standing next to Dr. Sandau is his surgical fellow, there to assist in the recovery of this heart. Another surgeon, Dr. Nathan Cohen, a notable Liver Transplant Surgeon, has joined the team and will be working in the abdominal cavity. He's there to procure the Liver, Pancreas and both kidneys for transplant on behalf of his partners and their recipients. He, too, has brought a transplant surgical fellow along to assist.

Among these professionals, these leaders in their chosen fields, it's certainly possible for tensions to build, egos to clash and spats to occur. But, when they enter the operating room together, for this purpose, all of that is left out in the scrub room. Each must work together to meet the needs of their recipients as a whole, not individually. If one of them needs more time to make sure the staging is right for their waiting recipient, then the others must allow for that to happen. Kevin, as the procurement coordinator, is the one man responsible for keeping each of them on time and on task. When he enters the room, each of the doctors anticipate the okay to begin.

The surgeons are standing in position around the operating table, the altar upon which JT will be offering his organs. Kevin approaches the foot of the table and asks, "Are we ready to begin?"

Each of them nod their approval and Dr. Sandau replies out loud, "Yes, Kevin, I believe we are. Have you heard from the recipient coordinators, are they each ready on their end?"

"Yes sir, they are. But, before we begin, we've been asked by Ms. Stone to have a moment of silence before the surgery begins. She has also given me a short statement to read."

Dr. Bankston says, "We've been doing this a lot lately. I'm not sure how I feel about it. I don't mean to be insensitive, but it's awfully personal, in nature."

"Martina, that's the whole point," Dr. Cohen interjects. "It's a short, solemn reminder that this is a life lost and that the family has entrusted us with his care and their final wishes for him."

"I understand that, it just tugs on my hearts strings a bit. Very well, carry on Kevin."

Kevin replies, "Thank you Dr. Bankston."

The room becomes silent and all the background activity stops as Kevin begins by saying, "On behalf of MDN, thanks to each of you that have gathered here for the procurement of JT's gifts." Reaching into his chest pocket, Kevin removes the folded piece of paper that Loretta gave him. He continues by saying, "His Mother, Loretta, has asked me to read this brief statement to you, to us, about him. It reads:

"My name is James Thomas Stone; my friends call me JT – so can you. I'm an eighteen-year-old boy who loved life and loved my family. My Mother, Loretta and my little brother, Mikey are my surviving family members.

*This is not how I expected to be remembered,
but I am willing to have this be my legacy. I was days
away from signing my letter of intent to play
basketball and attend the University of Kentucky,
even though my Mom wanted me to go play pro ball
in Europe. She and I didn't agree on this, but
ultimately, I just wanted to do what was best for all of
us. That's the kind of guy I was.*

*I'm asking each of you in this room to remember
me as a giving young man, willing to offer myself to
others so that they can live on. It is my hope that they
will each live long happy lives and honor me by doing
that."*

The room remained quiet for a few more minutes as the words written by Loretta hung in the air. Each of the procurement team members reflected on his sacrifice and the loss Loretta and her family must be feeling. Hardly ever, before this Moment of Silence practice started, were the procurement team members aware of the personal details of the donor. By doing this they now have an emotional connection to the donor and have more of a personal investment in the success of the donation.

As Kevin finished reading the written words, he folded the paper again and tucked it away in the same pocket. He said aloud, "That was the first time that I know of that a family member wrote their words as if spoken by the donor."

"That was touching, thank you for reading that to us," Dr. Bankston lamented.

"I couldn't agree more," Kevin said. Glancing at the digital clock on the wall, assuring that the time to begin was upon them, Kevin says, "Okay team, you may begin."

With that, two scalpels were skillfully passed to Drs. Sandau and Cohen. Each of them presses the razor-sharp blade to JT's skin; on his chest by Dr. Sandau and on his abdomen by Dr. Cohen. The surgeons press down into the skin and slide the blades downward making a vertical incision. This movement causes a single stream of blood to ooze from each of the cuts. The two incisions would be joined to make a long one from the top of his chest to the bottom of his abdomen. It had begun.

CHAPTER 30

The procurement surgery is well underway. The chest and abdominal cavities are fully open, using cavity spreading devices, allowing complete access to each organ system. The surgeons are elbow to elbow around the narrow table, respectful of each other's space as they prepare their individual organs for procurement. The five-liter frigid preservation solution bags hang from tall IV poles, ready to infuse through tubing lines that lead directly onto the surgical field. These will be used to flush the blood vessels and the organs free of JT's blood at just the appropriate time during the surgical procedure.

Kevin approaches the head of the bed and peeks over the drape that separates the sterile field from the rest of the area around the table. He asks, "How you guys doing in there? Are we getting close to cross clamp?"

Dr. Bankston, impatient as always, replies, "I've been ready."

In a controlled, monotone voice, Dr. Sandau replies, "Yes, the chest organs are ready. How much more time do you need Dr. Cohen?"

Dr. Cohen raises his head from his work, scans the room for a clock and notices the time. He, then, addresses the other surgeons, "Sorry, I'm just finishing up some extra dissection before we flush. But, I'm ready for cross clamp now."

Still a bit on the impatient side of things, Dr. Bankston asks the scrub tech, "Is the slushy-ice up on the field yet?"

Dr. Cohen, interjects, "There are two basins of ice down here, Martina, ready to go."

She looks at Kevin, over her custom-fitted surgical eye glasses, and says, "Then, it seems we're ready."

Two large aortic clamps are passed onto the field and into the hands of Drs. Sandau and Cohen. Individually, they place these clamps around the appropriate vessels in the chest and abdomen. With precise timing, they each squeeze their clamp shut on the appropriate vessels, preventing blood from moving past them. Suction catheters are then strategically placed in the cavities. The left atrial appendage of the heart is scissor clipped by Dr. Sandau and Dr. Cohen does the same to the venous return in the abdomen. Bright red blood begins to spill from the openings and the suction catheters begin to pull the blood out of the cavity and into the collection jars located near the foot of the bed.

Kevin has moved into position near the preservation fluid bags. Recognizing the venting of the blood from the vessels, Dr. Sandau gives the instruction, "Okay Kevin, start the flush." As Kevin slides open the roller clamps on all the preservation solution lines, Dr. Cohen passes a slush filled basin up to Dr. Bankston and they each pour the icy solution into their respective cavities. She looks up at Jamie, still at the head of the bed monitoring JT's vitals and instructs him, "Please decrease the tidal volume by two hundred and continue to ventilate during the procurement. I'll tell you when to stop. I want the lungs partially full of oxygen during transport." Jamie verbally acknowledges her order.

Kevin glances down at his watch and announces to the room, "Cross clamp is at ten-thirty-three." He, then, visually assures that the preservation solution is flowing quickly into the tubing, through the vessels and clearing the organs of blood.

While attending to the ventilator as instructed by Dr. Bankston, Jamie studies the vital signs monitor and watches as the heart rate slows dramatically and the rhythm changes to one of a slow wide-complex, then finally to a flat line. JT's heart has taken its final beats. In approximately ninety minutes, after being sewn in, re-perfused with oxygenated blood and stimulated with electricity this heart will beat again in a different man's chest, providing life to another – the medical miracle of organ donation. Jamie leans in toward JT's exposed face, which has lost its natural color and changed to an ashen hue due to the exsanguination that has just occurred. He whispers into JT's ear, "Rest in peace."

Loretta and Trina have moved to the high back chairs across the waiting room. Loretta, now an expert in waiting room etiquette, waited for the perfect opportunity to snag the most comfortable chairs in the place. Rather than discuss what was happening a few rooms away from them, they chose an alternate distraction. They've spent the last couple hours thumbing through gossip magazines that Trina has been collecting in her purse. Three spent ones lay on the floor between them as they each thumb through another rag.

Unnoticed at first, Kevin sidles up to them and places his belongings on the floor. Loretta catches his movement out of the corner of her eye and looks up to see him standing before her. His presence can mean only one thing to Loretta; her breathing becomes labored and tears begin to pool in her eyes. Kevin takes a knee in front of her chair and grabs her hands.

She asks, "They're all done?"

Kevin tightens his lips and gives a nod in the affirmative.

"Everything went well," he confirmed.

"He's okay now, right," she asks in a weaker, sad voice.

He gently replied, "I've made sure of it."

Trina stands and goes to Loretta's side to comfort her grieving friend.

Kevin slowly stands up and reaches for his bag and

white lab coat. Noticing his change in position, Loretta asks him, "So, I guess you're done then?"

"Unless you need me to stay, I should be going."

Loretta shoots a supportive glace up toward Trina. She looks back at Kevin and says, "I'll be okay." Grasping for Trina's hand, on her shoulder, Loretta continues, "We've got each other now."

Loretta lowers her head and begins to sob. The events of the last forty-eight hours begin to play out in her head with vivid detail. For Loretta, her life will forever be divided into two parts; before and after the death of her first-born son. Life in the "Before Era" was not exactly peaches, but it was full of hope for better days to come. How life goes for her in the "After Era" is now all up to her. She has peace in her soul because she knows what's guiding her, what's driving her. It's the promise that she made to JT, to ensure that he was proud of her and to provide for Mikey in the best way possible. It will be up to her to navigate her new course, using the Light she discovered in the chapel on the first floor of University Hospital.

CHAPTER 31

The meticulously manicured front yard of her parent's estate home is adorned with a large fountain in the middle of the circle driveway. As Kevin pulls up the long driveway, he shakes his head and mutters to himself, "It's hard to feel sorry for someone with a fountain in their yard. Really roughing it here, Sherry."

He pulls his car around the circle drive and stops as close to the front door as possible. Despite his fatigue, he bounds out of the car and begins walking, with purpose, up the front steps. He springs onto the porch and raps on the front door. Impatiently, he looks through the front window as the door opens, slowly, to reveal Sherry Mills.

"Kevin, what are you doing here? I thought you were going to call first?"

"Sorry for just showing up. I can't take it any longer, can we please talk?"

In a soft, welcoming voice she says, "Yes, of course." Sherry closes the door behind her and takes a seat on the front porch swing.

Kevin slides in next to her on the swing and pulls in a deep cleansing breath. He begins with, "Sherry, there's something I have to know before we talk about anything.

And, I need you to please be honest." He takes another long pause, perhaps delaying his pain. In his mind, living in ignorance would be better than the knowledge that she was capable of having an affair. The answer is unknown and he's not quite sure he could handle the worst-case scenario. He finally blurts it out, "Is there someone else?"

She quickly and defensively replies, "What? No! Why would you..."

Kevin interrupts her, "Be honest, please."

After a long, painful pause, she laments, "Well...okay. There was a guy from college who reached out to me on Facebook." The shame is surfacing in her voice, "I was feeling lonely, so I met up with him a couple times for lunch."

Controlled anger begins to mount. The real question has yet to be answered. He fires back, "Yeah, you were seen."

"By whom?"

"Not important. But, what is important is what happened." There it is, the question he needed answered.

She pleaded with him, "Nothing happened, Kevin. I promise."

Sherry leans forward in her seat, on the verge of tears, she covers her face.

He continued his questioning, "Then why are you upset right now? Feeling guilty?"

She sits up and looks into his face, "No, I don't feel guilty. I feel shame." She begins to cry. "I didn't fail to meet your standards, I failed to meet mine."

His soul aches for her as he sees her raw emotion. Kevin reaches for her hand. Before he touches her, she reaches for his. Their fingers interlock and their eyes meet. Sherry asks, "Can you please forgive me?"

Kevin has always been an old softy when it comes to Sherry. He has known all along, in his heart, that she wasn't capable of such a thing. He just needed to hear it from her. He shares his smile with her and says, "There's nothing to forgive. As far as I'm concerned, you had lunch with an old friend who will remain an old friend. Right?"

Sherry smiles back at him, through her tears. They embrace on the swing. "Right," she confirms.

A huge weight has been lifted off Kevin's heart, he can feel the relief and it's evident in his smiling face. As far has he's concerned, that issue has been resolved. Knowing that there is another major issue between them, Kevin searches for a way to introduce the matter. He begins by saying, "I just finished that case from yesterday."

"I can see that. You're still in your scrubs."

"He was an eighteen-year-old boy." Kevin begins to struggle containing his emotions but he fights through and continues, "I know his mother, she works at the diner by the office. Actually, I'd say we're friends."

"That's what you said yesterday, that's awful. I'm so sorry."

"Because of his sacrifice, her consent and the effort of a team of transplant professionals, six people's lives are saved." He stops to let his point resonate with her. "That's what I am, Sherry. That is the career I have chosen."

She retorts, "That may be what you are, but that's not who you are." She reaches up to touch Kevin's face, then continues, "You're my husband, and I want you to be the Father to our children. But, that can't happen if you're not around. My Dad wasn't around for us because he was always traveling for work." She gestures to their lush surroundings, "Yeah sure, he provided for us. But, this big house, the one before it and all this stuff will never replace the time we missed with him. I don't want our kids to have that same experience."

Kevin, with the excitement of a kid on Christmas, recognizes the prime opportunity to share his news. "They won't," he announces. An undisputable assurance in his voice comes through as he continues, "I told you that I was working on a solution to that problem. Well, it happened. You're looking at the new Manager of Clinical Procurement! Normal hours, a normal schedule!"

"Are you serious? When, when does this happen?"

"It's kind of a bittersweet moment, but, I just finished my last case."

Sherry jumps to her feet with excitement. She exclaims, "So, it's just us now? No more middle of the night calls? No more lonely nights without you?"

Kevin grabs her hands and pulls her back onto the swing. He says, "Baby, I'm too tired to dance, but yes, it's going to be different from here on out."

Sherry pivots her hips on the swing to face Kevin and grabs his hands and looks deeply into his eyes. "Your strength amazes me, it always has. You're the most kind, caring...," Sherry pauses to gently touch his chin, then continues, "Forgiving man I know." She slides both of her arms around his neck and continues, "I am so proud of you and the gifts you have...and that you share those with people you don't even know."

Kevin drops to his knees and places his head in Sherry's lap and begins to cry, tears of joy. He raises his eyes to meet hers, and says, "Please come home."

Sherry runs her fingers through his hair and begins to beam through her tears. She admits, "My bags are right behind that door."

CHAPTER 32

FOUR MONTHS LATER

Bright lights illuminate the small bathroom as Loretta stares deeply into her own eyes, the reflection in the clean mirror. She brings a small brush to her left eye and finishes applying a touch of mascara. A smile of deep satisfaction comes over her as she says aloud, "Okay Loretta, let's go do this."

She exits her master bedroom and quickly strolls down a bright hallway. Pictures of Mikey and JT adorn the walls. She stops and sticks her head in Mikey's room, asking, "Are you about ready to go?" He's not in there, so she keeps trekking down the hallway, loudly asking, "Mikey, are you ready?"

No response.

She enters the family room to find him playing a video game on the television. An assortment of boxes, both sealed and opened, are scattered about the room. It's bright and refreshingly new. A lone wall decoration hangs in the family room; it's a shadow box proudly displaying JT's MDN donor medal and an eight-by-ten photo of him, his senior picture. The sisters-in-life completed their project.

Mikey notices his mom enter the room and quickly takes

his gaze off the TV long enough to acknowledge her, he says, "Wow, Mommy, you look so pretty."

"Thanks baby. And, I love your jersey, it turned out really nice." He's wearing a much smaller version of JT's jersey that Tanya customized for him. She goes on, "Are you about ready to go? We don't want to be late."

"Can I finish this game," he asks.

"No baby, we've got to get going. Can you save it for later? Maybe you can show me how to play, okay?"

Loretta and Mikey exit the front door of their new, small duplex home. The "FOR RENT" sign still sits in the front yard. "Remind me to take that sign down later, please," she asks.

"Here, I'll get it now." Mikey snatches it from the ground and sets it inside the open garage.

"Well, thank you, Son. That's very helpful."

They hurriedly make their way to her car that's parked on the driveway. Loretta says quietly, to herself, "A new-used car is next." She glances toward the heavens and smiles. "Maybe an SUV."

As they climb into the car, Mikey asks, "Is Auntie Tanya meeting us there?"

"Knowing her, she's probably already there."

Loretta has successfully carried out the promise that she made to herself in that hospital chapel. She has enriched herself and their lives by making a few simple changes. As a result, Mikey has shown improvement in every aspect of his life and it's obvious to everyone around them. By changing her focus, she has opened the door to a new life for them.

As Loretta pulls her car onto the driveway of Kevin Mills' home, she notices that the setting sun has painted the Springtime sky with an orange-red hue. Even that would have gone unnoticed six months ago. She says, "Look at that sky, Mikey."

"Yes, it's beautiful," he responds.

They exit the vehicle and hustle toward the front door. Mikey asks, "Can I push the button?"

"Just once this time. Let's not repeat the past," recalling their last visit to The Mills' home.

The front door opens and Kevin is standing before them. Through the screen door he welcomes them inside. Mikey reaches up and pulls the screen door open for his mother. Kevin notices the gesture and comments, "My, what a little gentleman."

"It's a work in progress, for both of us," Loretta reports, with a wink and a smile.

As they enter the foyer, Sherry Mills emerges from the living room. She's in a form-fitting summer dress, revealing her small baby-bump. With open arms, Sherry says, "Oh

Loretta, it's so good to see you again." They share a quick hug, and Sherry continues, "We love it when you visit." She bends at the waist to greet Mikey, saying, "I hope you like barbecued hotdogs and ice cream."

Mikey smiles and nods his approval.

Loretta, holding Sherry's extended hands, says, "Well, don't you look beautiful in that dress?" She hesitates but slowly reaches for Sherry's protruding belly, "May I?"

"I'm starting to get used to it. Kevin, does it constantly," Sherry says as she shoots her husband an approving laugh.

"Best moments of my day," he admits.

Sherry turns and walks toward the living room in an effort to lead their guests, saying, "Follow me. Everyone's in here."

Loretta pauses to look at the wedding picture on the wall and admits to Kevin, "I just love this photo."

With a deep sigh of relief, Kevin says, "Me too Loretta, me too."

As Mikey follows Sherry into the family room, Kevin reaches for Loretta's arm and pulls her close to share a moment. He asks her, "Have you given any more thought to coming to work for me at MDN? Your interview was great and we really think it's a perfect fit."

"I was going to tell you later, but I guess now is as good a time as any. Yes, I accept. I'm looking forward to working with Melanie, and for you. It feels so right." Hardly able to contain her excitement, she continues, "It's an opportunity to tell JT's story, carry on his legacy and help other families."

"Excellent choice! Everyone in the office will be so happy."

She leans into him and softly says, "What you have done for me and my family, I just can't tell you how much it means to us all."

"Please don't...," he mutters before being cut off by Loretta.

"Especially this, I've been waiting for this moment for months. I finally get to meet him."

Kevin offers out his bent arm to lead Loretta. "Right this way, my friend."

The two of them enter the family room to find the other invited guests; Tanya is in a conversation with Bryan and Trina Kelley. Bryan is sitting up straight and tall in his chair. He's without the oxygen tubing that used to adorn his face. He has regained his strength, his color, his life.

Mikey has already found his way into his Auntie's arms.

Loretta, with a touch of apprehension, approaches Trina and Bryan. He rises up to his feet, tall and strong, towering over the people around him. Trina steps forward and gives Loretta a strong hug. Their embrace allows for a private exchange. Trina whispers, "Hello, Sister," followed by a tighter squeeze.

With glassy eyes, Loretta admits to her, "I'm a little scared."

"He's a big man, but he doesn't bite." They both giggle as they release their hold on each other, but not completely, as they continue to hold hands; it's Loretta's safety blanket.

In a rather proud moment, Trina says, "I can't believe I'm finally getting to say this. Loretta, I want you to meet my husband, Bryan."

Bryan extends his right hand toward Loretta. Likewise, she extends hers and they engage in a cordial handshake. He mutters, "I told myself I wasn't going to cry."

"Me too. But, I lied," Loretta confesses. Her eyes begin to fill with tears as she sees the living embodiment of her son's sacrifice.

Unable to contain his appreciation any longer, Bryan blurts out, "Can I please hug you? My words just won't be enough to express my gratitude." Without a single word, mostly because she can't formulate one, Loretta opens her arms to Bryan. They embrace and each begin to cry tears of joy and appreciation.

The sound of silence echoes through the room.

Mikey takes his place at Loretta's side and she reaches down to put her hand on his shoulder, as she and Bryan fully release their embrace. She looks down toward Mikey and says, "Son, this is the man I told you about. Bryan is my friend Trina's husband."

Innocent and unapologetic, Mikey says, "He doesn't look sick, Momma."

Wiping tears from his cheeks, Bryan says, "Well, I'm not sick anymore buddy. Your brother saved my life. You know, he saved many lives?"

"Yeah, he's my hero."

Bryan, gingerly, takes a knee to look eye-to-eye with Mikey. "He's mine too. You know, you and your Mommy are heroes too."

"We are?"

Bryan explained, "You gave so others, including me, could live." Mikey gives his Mother's waist a tight squeeze and then hides his face in that familiar spot behind her back. Bryan slowly stands up, with Trina's help, and addresses Loretta again, "You know, JT may be gone but he'll always live on in me; as long as there is air in these lungs." Loretta's eyes begin watering again as she pulls Bryan in for another tight hug.

Kevin, unnoticed, walks toward the fireplace mantle to retrieve his stethoscope. He says, "Bryan, would you mind if she listened now?"

"Not at all," he replied.

Loretta turns and gives a puzzled look to Kevin and asks, "Listen? Listen to what?"

"The sound of his lungs working. Just listen to the air moving in and out."

This takes Loretta by surprise. She, breathlessly, asks, "Can I?"

Kevin places the earpieces of the stethoscope into her ears. He, then, places the bell onto Bryan's chest as Loretta listens, intently. Kevin explains, "These lungs are just one of JT's gifts."

Bryan takes in a full prideful breath and exhales. Loretta's mouth opens as she hears the amplified air movement inside Bryan's chest. He takes in another deep breath as tears stream from her eyes.

"Can you hear that," Kevin inquires.

Loretta, joyfully replies, "That's my boy!"

Loretta removes the stethoscope from her ears and lays her head against Bryan's chest. Trina joins, and the three share a tearful embrace.

THE END

EPILOGUE
THREE MONTHS LATER

For Loretta, the transition to the Missouri Donor Network has been a gratifying and smooth one. Her last day of work at the Forum City Diner was bittersweet, however. On one hand, she was moving into to a "real job," as she liked to call it. She was making much more money, a consistent income. Her hours were normal and they worked much better in accommodating the needs of her youngest, Mikey. On the other hand, she was leaving her best friend behind. But, a change in careers will never affect their relationship; after all, they are now sisters-in-life.

The team at MDN has welcomed her with open arms and she has quickly become a favorite around the office. Although still in orientation, she has been able to make a meaningful and compassionate impact on the families with whom she has worked as a Family Support Liaison. Melanie has taken Loretta under her wing and has been teaching her all about the difficult job that she accepted. Another benefit to this new position is that she gets to see Kevin Mills on a more consistent basis. Loretta's not slinging much coffee these days, but will still delver a cup to Kevin every once in a while. Only now, she won't accept his tips.

On this day, it was Kevin who paid a visit to Loretta at her desk, located in "The Pit"; the Family Support Staff section of the office. Holding two cups of coffee with one hand, he gently knocks on the cubicle wall partition.

"To what do I owe this honor," she says as she reaches out to accept the cup of joe.

"I thought I'd check on you to see how everything is going. How's Mikey doing?"

With a bright smile she replies, "You know, he's doing really well. We talk about JT a lot and I think it helps him. The counselors at his school have kept a close eye on him and tell me that he has done really well. And, the great reports continue from the summer day sports program he is attending."

"I'm so glad to hear that, Loretta. He is such a good boy and you've done a great job seeing him through this."

"Thank you, Kevin. That really means a lot to me, coming from you. We've also been able to spend a little time with Trina and Bryan Kelley. I think, more than anything, seeing how well Bryan is progressing has helped Mikey – and me, for that matter. It's such an amazing thing that happened. A true miracle."

"I couldn't agree more," Kevin says as he puts his cup on her desk. "Do you mind if I sit down with you for a minute," he asks her while pulling up a chair next to her desk.

"No, not at all. What's up?"

"How about you? How are you doing," he asks.

"I have my moments, but not in front of him. My depression is getting better, my grief counselor has made the difference."

"Kevin says, "I'm so happy to hear that."

"Working here has helped a lot too."

"Even better. I know that we love having you here with us." Kevin reaches into his sports coat and removes an envelope from the inside pocket. He says, "I have something for you. Normally, this is mailed to each of the donor families a few months after the donation is completed. But, I asked the staff to hold this back from the mailing so that I could hand deliver it to you."

"Is that what I think it is," she asks.

"Yes, it's the official letter notifying you of the gifts that JT provided through his organ donation. It also gives a brief description of the people whose lives were affected by JT's generosity."

Loretta takes a moment to look at the family portrait on the corner of her desk. A tear wells up in the inside corner of her eye and she reaches for a tissue. She says, "I have been wondering about this but didn't want to overstep my bounds."

Handing the envelope to Loretta, Kevin says, "Here you go. I'll give you some privacy."

"No, Kevin, please don't go. It would mean a lot to me to share this moment with you. After all, I wouldn't be here and none of this would have happened without you. Please stay. In fact, I don't think I'll be able to get through it. Will you please read it to me?"

"Are you sure, Loretta," he asks. "Maybe you should open this with Mikey."

"No, I need to know what's in there before I share it with him. He's been doing so well, I don't want anything to change that."

"Well, maybe you're right. I'd be happy to read it with you," Kevin replies as he adjusts his seat so that he is facing Loretta directly.

He begins to read the two-page letter in a warm, tender, heartfelt tone; one that Loretta will forever remember as she learns the fate of each of the intended recipients of JT's gifts of life.

The letter reads:

> *"Dear Ms. Loretta Stone,*
> *We, at Missouri Donor Network, would like to thank you for the loving gifts that were provided by you through the organ donation from your son, James*

Thomas(JT) Stone. His donation of seven organs saved the lives of six people. His lungs, while transplanted as a pair into one recipient, count as two individual organs because they could be separated and used to serve two recipients.

JT's heart saved the life of a fifty-two-year-old male. He has recovered well from his transplant and expects to return to work as soon as possible. He is married with three children and six grandchildren, with another one on the way. He is an avid tennis player and loves to spend his extra time volunteering at the VA Hospital, as he is a US Army Veteran. He, and his family, wish to extend their "heart-felt" thank you.

JT's lungs saved the life of a forty-three-year-old male. He has made an impressive recovery from his double-lung transplant. He is married and intends to enjoy his gift of life by helping others as they fight their battles with organ disease. He also intends to donate his spare time volunteering with organ procurement organizations, including MDN.

JT's liver saved the life of a twenty-eight-year-old female. Her full recovery has been delayed by a short bout of rejection, which was treated and she is expected to make a full recovery. She is a newly married, fourth-grade school teacher. She plans to return to work next school year. She wishes to share with you her plans to honor your son's donation by providing education regarding organ and tissue donation to her students and members of her local school district.

One of JT's kidneys and his pancreas saved the life of a forty-six-year-old male. He has made a fantastic recovery and is currently no longer receiving hemodialysis and he is no longer requiring three times a day insulin injections. He wishes to share with you his gratitude for drastically changing his quality of life. As a single father of two grown sons, he plans to travel the country now that he is not tethered to a dialysis machine, keeping him alive.

JT's other kidney saved the life of an eighteen-year-old female. She is recovering well after her transplant. She is grateful for the opportunity she now has to pursue her college education at The University of Kentucky in the Fall.

Once again, we appreciate the opportunity to assist you in your desire to help others in need through the life-saving gift of organ donation."

After Kevin finishes reading the final words of the letter,

he looks up to find Loretta beaming with pride as joy-filled tears stream down her checks. He sets the letter on the surface of her desk, and says, "Loretta, that is one impressive letter."

She lifts the letter from the desk as she dries her eyes with a tissue. She begins to skim the typed words and flips to the last page. Surprised, she looks up at Kevin and says, "This is signed by you. That's your name on here."

"Yes, as the coordinator of record for JT's donation, it was my responsibility to gather that information and provide it to you. We do that for each of our cases."

Loretta stands up and offers Kevin her hands, asking him to join her. He stands and they share a warm embrace. Kevin says, over her shoulder. "Apparently, JT will be attending UK after all."

Loretta laughs and slaps Kevin on the shoulder. She then pulls him in for a tighter hug, saying, "Thanks to you."

About the Author

Robert Horsey is a critical care registered nurse who has dedicated most of his eighteen-year career to the field of Organ Donation and Transplantation. He has held the positions of Interventional Organ Procurement Coordinator with Mid-America Transplant Services, located in St. Louis, Missouri; Clinical Transplant Coordinator with St. Vincent Indianapolis Hospital's Heart Transplant Program and Clinical Transplant Coordinator with Indiana University Health - University Hospital's Liver Transplant Program, both located in Indianapolis, Indiana. Currently, Robert is on staff at the Indiana Donor Network as an Organ Recovery Coordinator.

He has held national certification as a Certified Procurement Transplant Coordinator (CPTC) and a Certified Clinical Transplant Coordinator (CCTC), as awarded by The American Board for Transplant Certification. Robert received his Bachelor of Science in Nursing degree (cum laude honors) from the University of Missouri – St. Louis, Barnes Hospital College of Nursing.

Robert is the last (along with his twin brother, Charlie) in the lineup of nine children. He currently resides in Carmel, Indiana with his girlfriend, Courtney and her two boys, Michael and Ozzy. And, yes, he and most of his siblings are die-hard and loyal St. Louis Cardinal Baseball Fans!!

Gifted is Robert's first novel.

www.gifted-thenovel.com